The Roguish Duke

HISTORICAL REGENCY ROMANCE NOVEL

Sally Forbes

Copyright © 2024 by Sally Forbes
All Rights Reserved.
This book may not be reproduced or transmitted in any form without the written permission of the publisher. In no way is it legal to reproduce, duplicate, or transmit any part of this document in either electronic means or in printed format. Recording of this publication is strictly prohibited and any storage of this document is not allowed unless with written permission from the publisher.

Table of Contents

Prologue 3
Chapter One 10
Chapter Two 16
Chapter Three 23
Chapter Four 29
Chapter Five 35
Chapter Six 43
Chapter Seven 51
Chapter Eight 59
Chapter Nine 65
Chapter Ten 72
Chapter Eleven 80
Chapter Twelve 84
Chapter Thirteen 94
Chapter Fourteen 100
Chapter Fifteen 110
Chapter Sixteen 117
Chapter Seventeen 123
Chapter Eighteen 131
Chapter Nineteen 140
Chapter Twenty 148
Chapter Twenty-One 153
Epilogue 159

Prologue

"I have decided that it is time for you to find a wife."

Joseph looked at his mother sidelong, rolling his eyes when she caught his gaze.

"Do not think that I will be put away from this idea!" she exclaimed, as he returned his attention to the paper he was attempting to read. It had been sent from London and he was eager to read all of the goings-on which had taken place over the Christmas season within society. "You have been the Duke of Yarmouth for five years now and as yet, you have done nothing to secure the family line!"

Barely giving his mother even the smallest bit of attention, Joseph waved one hand vaguely in her direction as the fire in the hearth crackled beside him. "Mother, I have two younger brothers. Both of them are more than suitable to take on the role, should I ever be displaced." It was not something that he was in the least bit worried about, however, for Joseph was hale and hearty and though he had an intention of marrying some day, he had no desire to do so at present.

"But you must!" she exclaimed, stalking across the drawing room and practically whipping the paper out of his hands. "It is required!"

Joseph scowled, disliking his mother's insistence. "Mother, that is quite enough. I have already made it plain that I *will* marry one day but it shall only be at the day and time of my choosing."

"No, it shall not be." The Duchess lifted her chin and gazed down at him with such a fire in her eyes that Joseph shifted in his chair, suddenly feeling a little unsettled. "Yarmouth, I have had quite enough of your laziness, your disinterest and your selfishness. The whispers about you are not good and society is well aware of your present reputation – a reputation which will soon become roguish should nothing change!"

"I have not been in London for the last few months, Mother, so I cannot imagine where you would get such an idea from." Though Joseph kept his voice mild, he tried to ignore the streak of worry which ran through him. Some months ago, he had decided that a very pretty young lady by the name of Lady Sara would be good for his next conquest and had set about it. The young lady had been rather reluctant, however, and though Joseph knew he ought to have stepped back, his determination to have her kisses brought about such a strength of force within him, he had promised her things that he had no intention of truly seeking out. It had all become rather sordid in the end and though he had managed to keep the truth from society – and had bribed those involved for their silence – he had chosen to return to his estate rather than linger in London. He had not heard if there had been any whispers about him in that time and part of him was a little loathe to find out. After all, he had spent a good deal of time attempting to make certain that the *ton* did not think of him as an utter scoundrel and he did not want that to change.

"I have heard of what is said of you from my friends and from those connected to our family," his mother stated, clearly refusing to let the matter drop. "I do not know your reasons for staying back from London but I can imagine they are nothing but selfish."

Joseph frowned. "That is a little inconsiderate of you, no?"

This did not have the desired effect upon his mother, however. She took in a deep breath, set her hands to her waist and then glared at him. "Either you seek a wife in London this Season in a few months' time, or I shall make your life nothing short of a misery."

Joseph blinked in astonishment, for his mother was always quiet and considered, never once speaking with the fierceness she did at present. "I – I beg your pardon?"

"I hardly think that I need to repeat myself," she replied, with that same determination in her voice which shocked Joseph utterly. "I am residing with you at present, just as I ought given that this is the house where I raised both your brothers and yourself when your dear father was alive. You know that I will only remove myself from this house when you marry, for I shall have the Dower house."

Anger flickered in Joseph's heart. "I could have you removed there whenever I please."

"Ah, but should you do so, then you will have society looking down upon you and I know very well that you want society – well, certain members of society, shall I say – to think *well* of you. It is not often that you go to London but when you do visit, you make certain to steal as much attention from young ladies as possible, you throw money away at the card table and yet I know you want the *ton* to think you an excellent sort, albeit a little rogue-like."

"I believe that my reputation is *my* business, Mother!"

She shook her head. "I fervently wish that such tidings were indeed true. You know that your reputation as the Duke is of vital importance and that how you are seen by society will directly impact upon not only myself but your brothers and their families, but that does not seem to concern you! You do not think of us and have seemingly no interest in the responsibilities that being a Duke represents. That is not the sort of gentleman your father thought you would be."

Joseph's hand curled into a fist and he thumped it, hard, on the arm of his chair, sending a jolt up through his arm. "How dare you say such a thing? You know very well that I have taken on this title with nothing but thoughts for my responsibilities!"

Despite the obvious upset and strain, his mother did not step back from what she had been saying. "You have *thought* of a good many things yes, I shall give you that. However, you do not seem to act! The crops, though they do well, should be reviewed in light of the new findings about crop rotation. Your tenants should have their houses reviewed and considered so that improvements might be made. You should consider the new business ventures that have been offered to you, rather than simply continuing on with what you have always known! And you should certainly stop pursuing various young ladies, all of whom will give you their affections until you become bored with them and move away from them!"

"How... " The anger began to fade as Joseph looked up at his mother. "How do you know such things?"

She laughed but it did not hold any mirth within it. "I have been Duchess for a very long time, my son. I am well acquainted with all that transpires within this household. You believe that the servants are loyal to you and yes, they are, but they also know that

I, as mistress of this house, have cause to know all that is taking place. And it does not take much effort to hear from the tenants just how little their houses have been considered these last two years; how the thatch is poor and weakening in some places, how the wind and the rain come through. Society is also very good at informing me of my son's poor behaviour to the young ladies, both here in our own vicinity and in London. That is a matter which cannot be kept to oneself."

A flush of shame began to burn up through Joseph's chest but he looked away rather than let her perceive it. That part, certainly, was true, loathe though he was to admit it. His tenants had not been something he had considered a good deal of late, given that he had become very taken up with his own estate. Joseph very much enjoyed being out of doors and spent a good deal of time there rather than inside in his study or his drawing room. Instead of writing letters, he much preferred to ride as far as he could before, eventually turning around. Business matters were set aside in favor of other outdoor sports and, thus far, Joseph had not seen any issue with it. His estate ran very well, his finances were good and his business affairs were all in order. Yes, he had not tried any new ventures, had assumed that his crops were doing well and had thought only of himself for much of the time but had that been truly such a bad thing?

"This is preposterous, Mother," he said, pulling himself out of his many thoughts and instead, determining not to permit his mother to do anything that she had threatened. "You have no right to state such things. I will do as I please and will marry as and when I so wish."

The Duchess shrugged. "Very well. Then, if you are determined to continue on in such a way, then I shall have no other choice but to do as I have threatened."

"Which is to make my life a misery."

She nodded. "Precisely."

"Then you are willing to manipulate me, to use me as you wish simply so that I will do as *you* ask?" Joseph got to his feet though his mother still did not move, did not even flicker. "You will force my hand?"

"Yes." The Duchess lifted her chin. "I am doing his because I must. I am tired of the Duke of Yarmouth being spoken of in society, tired of hearing that I only have two dutiful sons rather than three. No, Yarmouth, you will come to London this Season and you will do as you must."

Joseph shook his head. "No, I will not."

His mother gazed back at him but Joseph held his gaze, willing to simply stare her down but, the longer that they looked at each other in silence, the more uncomfortable he became. The Duchess did not falter, gazing at him with her chin lifted a notch and a sharpness in her eyes which he had never seen before. Swallowing hard, Joseph looked away and then let out a slow breath, despising the situation that he was now facing.

"I warn you now, it will be more miserable than you have ever experienced."

The whisper from his mother made Joseph shudder though he tried to hide it. He had always known the Duchess to be a sweet-natured lady, had often admired her kindness and her sweetness but now, it seemed, her nature had changed entirely! *And all because she has decided I must wed.*

"This is unfair," he stated, swiping through the air between them with both hands. "How can you utter such a thing? You have never comported yourself or expressed such sentiments towards me until now!"

His mother's lips quirked, though her eyebrows flung themselves down. "I have said nothing for the last five years but now, the time has come for me to be honest with you. I want to know that the family line is secure and that you are taking the responsibility your father gave you with the upmost seriousness."

"By threatening to injure me?"

The smile returned. "Oh, I did not say that I would injure you, did I? I said that I would make your life a little more... difficult than it has been before. Perhaps then that might take you out of the way of thinking only of yourself and might, I hope, force you to reconsider your responsibilities, yes?"

Joseph did not know what to do. On one hand, his mother had no right to speak to him in such a way as this and *he* had every right to stop her from doing so but on the other, given that he did not know what it was she intended to do, it would not be as simple as asking her to desist! A thought came to him and with a quirk of his lips, he held her gaze steadily. This was his mother! His mother, who had never once raised her voice to him, who had always done everything she could to please those within her household and those outside of it also. She could not – would not – do such a thing as this! This was a pretense, surely? It was nothing he could take seriously, not when he knew her as he did. It was only words, words meant to force him into action. "I am afraid, Mother, that I do not believe you."

This made his mother's eyes flash and Joseph's smile stuck to his lips, no longer as confident in his belief as he had been before. "Is that so?"

"I... yes, it is." Joseph lifted his chin and held her gaze steadily. "I do not think that you would do such a thing to me. I am sure that you have said such a thing in order to force my hand but I will not be moved, I am afraid. Your threats shall not take root with me."

This brought a lengthy silence between them and, at the end of it, the Duchess began to nod slowly, pulling her gaze away from him. "Very well," she said, her voice low and quiet as a sense of triumph began to flood through Joseph. Had he been correct in his belief after all? Had she, indeed, said such things in the hope of merely pushing him into action?

"I appreciate that you are concerned for me but I can assure you, you need not be. I am more than able to do what is required of me but it will be at a time of my choosing."

His mother nodded but then gave him a long look, one finger rubbing lightly across her lips, her thumb at her chin.

"I am glad we had this conversation," Joseph continued, not quite certain what else to say. "Now, the paper if you do not mind?"

The Duchess glanced away before picking up the paper in her hands and walking across the room, rather than giving it to him. "You presume me to be insignificant, feeble and devoid of resolve," she articulated, quickly feeding the paper to the fire as Joseph let out an exclamation of upset, half out of his chair again as his mother turned her gaze to him once more. "You will see that I am not, Yarmouth. Your father is no longer here to make certain that you do your duty and therefore, it now rests with me given that you do not do such a thing yourself! I had thought that you, as the eldest, would do what was asked but instead I see that it is quite the opposite and I am ashamed of you. I *am* shamed by what the *ton* knows of you; your lack of diligence in business matters, the complaints of your tenants and your fleeting interest in various ladies of the *ton*. Something must change and if you do not do that for yourself, then believe me when I say that I will force it upon you regardless."

Before Joseph could say anything, the lady had taken her leave of him, leaving the only sound the crackling of the fire as it burnt up the last parts of the newspaper. It had only been a small act, something insignificant really, but it had shocked Joseph right to his very core. This was not someone that he recognized! His mother had never done or said such things before and now, unfortunately, Joseph was slowly beginning to believe that all she had said, she would do.

"I will *not* find a wife," he muttered to himself, his hands curling into fists again as he fought to find a fresh determination within himself. "I have no interest in matrimony, no desire to take a wife." Lifting his chin, he nodded to himself. "And I certainly shall *not* be forced into it."

Chapter One

"Good evening, Your Grace! How pleasant to see you here this evening."

Joseph offered his host a smile, all the while feeling himself more than a little heavy-hearted. "Good evening, Lord Umbridge. How very kind of you to extend an invitation to both myself and my mother."

"But of course, of course!" Lord Umbridge gestured to the ballroom. "I am sure that many within society will be glad to see you present, Your Grace. Allow me a few moments of conversation with your mother before I release her to join you, yes?"

Joseph nodded, his back stiff and his shoulders pulled back as he walked toward the ballroom. He had very little to say to his mother at the present moment and would be very glad indeed if Lord Umbridge wished to talk with her for the rest of the evening! Given what he knew of his mother and what she intended for him this evening, he had no genuine desire to spend any further time in her company.

"Good evening, Your Grace!" A voice filled with surprise caught his attention and Joseph turned his head, looking down into a pair of gentle brown eyes. "I did not think you would be coming to London so early in the Season."

"Nor did I, Lady Newforth." Joseph bowed towards the lady, recognizing her to be one of those he had captured in his arms only a few months ago, though given that she was widowed, he did not think that to be particularly grievous. "However, I have come to London to – " He stopped short, realizing that he had no desire whatsoever to inform the lady that he was here to find himself a wife. The truth was, he had no interest in that at all but it was because of the heavy weight of his mother's insistence that he had finally given in. "I have come to London to enjoy the good company found here," he finished saying, as the lady's eyes glowed. "I do hope I make myself clear?"

She touched his arm for a moment, moving just a little closer. "Yes, you do indeed," she murmured, practically purring as a faint stirring in Joseph's core reminded him about all they had shared. "Mayhap you might –"

***

"My son is here to find a bride, Lady Newforth."

Joseph closed his eyes, his jaw tightening as his mother came to stand directly beside him, clearly aware of what sort of conversation she had stumbled upon. "Mother, I think –"

"Did I not hear that you were recently engaged, Lady Newforth?" the Duchess continued, ignoring Joseph completely. "You must tell me his name, for I have quite forgotten!"

A cold hand began to wrap around Joseph's heart as he looked to Lady Newforth, seeing her turn her gaze away as color hit her cheeks. He had always promised himself that he would never capture a lady in his arms who was already spoken for and yet, now it seemed that he had come dangerously close to doing so.

"Yes, to the Earl of Chesterfield." Lady Newforth licked her lips, glancing over her shoulder as though she thought to spy the very person she was speaking of. "It was only very recent and –"

"My congratulations to you both," the Duchess interrupted, shooting an angry look towards Joseph who only shook his head, words of protest on his lips but remaining unspoken. "Do excuse us, Lady Newforth, if you would. My son is to take me to find Lady Wigton and we must depart here at once."

Joseph had no other choice but to take his mother's arm and lead her away from Lady Newforth, though he did find himself a little relieved to no longer be in the lady's company. He had not known that she was engaged and certainly would not have even *thought* to engage in any sort of flirtation with the lady had he been aware. He cleared his throat, glancing to his mother who was walking with her head held high but a spot of color in her cheeks.

"I did not know she was betrothed, Mother," he said quietly, realizing that he had no need to explain himself to her but finding the desire to do so sitting within him regardless. "I was entirely unaware of it."

She shook her head but kept her gaze directly ahead of her,

not looking up at him. "I do not know whether or not I can believe that. Your reputation is not exactly pristine, is it?"

Joseph scowled. "I have always told myself that I would never engage in any manner of flirtation with a lady who was attached to a gentleman. Whether you believe that or not is none of my concern." He sniffed as she looked up at him, ignoring the anger in her eyes. Things between his mother and himself had become strained the last few months and though he abhorred the weakness within himself which had given in to her demands and had finally consented to find a bride, he also was looking forward to the moment that he would be granted relief from it all.

"There is Lady Wigton." His mother directed him with a point of one finger. "Now, you know that I am to introduce you to her daughter, Lady Hannah. You will behave well, I hope."

"You do not have to speak to me as though I am a child," Joseph muttered, a little frustrated with his mother's attitude. "I am well able to behave well in society, I assure you."

"I am yet to become convinced of that," came the quick reply, though Joseph could not respond given that Lady Wigton turned to greet them both. He bowed and forced a smile, finding himself a little relieved that the lady appeared to be standing alone and was not with her daughter, only for the lady to then beckon to someone behind him.

"Come now, Hannah, come and greet the Duchess of Yarmouth and her son, the Duke of Yarmouth."

Joseph had no choice but to turn and look as a young lady detached herself from a smaller group of ladies and came obediently towards her mother. She was, Joseph considered, not particularly beautiful but not overly plain either, which he appreciated. There was no spark in her eyes but her brown curls glinted copper in the candlelight.

"Your Grace, it is a delight to see you again."

Joseph blinked quickly, then inclined his head as a frown marred his forehead. He had no recollection of ever meeting this young lady and yet, evidently, she seemed to be aware of him. With a cough, he lifted his head and looked back into her eyes, though there was a glint in her eye and a slight pull to her mouth that Joseph did not much like.

"Of course, Lady Hannah." He tried to smile but his mouth refused to pull into it. "I hope you are enjoying this evening?"

She tilted her head just a little, her mouth flattening. "Very much. Will you be in attendance for a considerable time?"

"I – yes, I intend to be here for some months," Joseph stammered, his words becoming a little muddled as he hid what he wanted to say, covering it with words he did not truly mean. "I have come with my mother, as you may perceive."

"And he is here to find himself a bride at long last!"

This declaration from his mother made Joseph's heart rip apart, dread flooding him as Lady Hannah snatched in a breath, her eyes rounding at the edges.

"That is not... that is to say –"

"Come now, my son, you need not be coy about it," the Duchess exclaimed, making Joseph's frustrations leap up all the more. "I shall be searching through the *ton* for those young ladies who might well be a suitable match for my son. He has deigned to permit me such a responsibility and I am already relishing the task!"

A rush of energy poured into Joseph's frame, urging him to hurry away, to step away from the conversation before she could say any more. "That is to say, I *may* consider matrimony," he added, hastily. "I am sure, Lady Wigton that you understand my mother's enthusiasm but it is given a little too hastily, I think."

This did nothing to dampen the excitement in the lady's expression and Joseph's heart sank, especially when she turned her head to face her daughter.

"That is most exciting, Your Grace! I am sure that your mother will be of the greatest help to you." She said all of this as she looked at her daughter, though Lady Hannah said nothing, her expression entirely unchanged. "Should you like to step out for a dance this evening? You will find many willing young ladies, I am sure!"

Joseph swallowed thickly, seeing that the lady was now hopeful – and expectant – that he might dance with her daughter this evening. "I do not think that I –"

"The quadrille, mayhap?" The Duchess broke in this time, sending Joseph a fiery glance which Joseph tried his best to ignore.

"Or the cotillion?"

"I am not certain that —"

This time, it was not Joseph who ignored the question but Lady Hannah instead. She drew herself up to her full height, looked back at him steadily and kept her chin lifted. "After what you did to my closest friend, Lady Sara, I have no interest in standing up with you."

"Hannah!" Lady Wigton exclaimed, only for Joseph's own mother to drop her head, her eyes closing tightly. There was a clear moment of tension as the small group all stood in tense silence, though Joseph's heart began to thud furiously, disliking Lady Hannah intensely. This was rudeness beyond measure, he mused inwardly, and from such a mere chit as this! His face began to burn though he kept Lady Hannah's gaze steadily.

"I do not think that what transpired between the lady and myself is anyone's business but my own."

"And you can say that in such a way as to make it plain that you have no responsibility!" Lady Hannah cried, making her mother exclaim again, trying to quieten her but to no avail. "You have tried to keep this to yourself, I know, for you do not want anyone else to be aware of it, but you stole her affections and promised her that you would marry — though you begged her to keep it a secret. And then what did you do? You turned your back on her and instead, found another lady to keep close instead. And this in the full knowledge that she had turned down two other gentlemen's offer of courtship in the belief that your proposal would soon come!"

There was nothing for him to say. He could not defend himself, not when he had done everything that the lady had just said. Nor could he say that he had truly had an intention of marrying the lady for that in itself had also been false. Lady Sara had been a distraction for him for a time, nothing more. He had only hoped that the news of this would never come to light.

"You cannot say a word against this, can you?" Lady Hannah laughed without mirth, her face contorted with anger, her eyes brimming with tears. "You are the very last gentleman I should ever stand up with and if I had my way, all of society would be warned about you so that none would ever come near you again."

With this, she twisted away from her mother and from

Joseph, hurrying through the crowd of guests as though she could not move fast enough to remove herself from him. Joseph did not know what to do, glancing around surreptitiously and realizing just how many people nearby had heard what Lady Hannah had put to him. A sense of mortification began to stir up within him, his chest and neck growing warm as he looked down to the ground, the only place he could avoid the gaze of anyone.

"I think I shall take myself to the card room," he said, in what he hoped was a nonchalant manner. "Do excuse me."

As he made his way from his mother's side, Joseph slowly became aware of the whispers which were beginning to spread out around him. It was as though every person present had not only heard what Lady Hannah had said but was now eager to speak about it, making the whispers grow all the stronger. Joseph had never once experienced shame over his behavior for he had always been careful to make sure that society was not fully aware of what he had been doing but now, for the very first time, that sensation began to wash over him. It was a most unpleasant one and Joseph scowled darkly, rubbing one hand over his forehead as he stepped out of the ballroom in search of the card room.

This was not going to be the Season that either he or his mother had anticipated, he realized. Instead, he was going to carry a heavy burden... and one that was entirely of his own making.

Chapter Two

"Did you hear about the Duke of Yarmouth?"

Louisa continued to sew quietly in the corner of the drawing room as her two sisters chattered mindlessly together. They had been talking about all manner of things in society though she, however, had very little interest in what was being said.

"There have always been whispers that he is nothing more than a rogue but I did not think he would behave as poorly as that!" Rachel continued, as Louisa glanced at her, before turning her attention back to her needle and embroidery thread. "Though he is a Duke, I suppose, so there will be someone within society wiling to marry him!"

"Marry him?" Ruth, the youngest of the sisters, let out a quiet laugh. "I am sure that there will be many a young lady eager to do such a thing but their mothers and fathers will be less inclined, I am sure, given what has been said. To know that he would treat that lady with such inconsideration is dreadful!"

"Though I did hear that she is now married and quite happily settled," came the reply, as a niggle of curiosity began to grow in Louisa's heart. "I did think it most astonishing that a Duke would think to behave in such a way, however. I thought that gentlemen with high titles were expected to behave with the greatest integrity!"

"It seems as though the Duke of Yarmouth lacks such integrity, unfortunately." Ruth sighed and shook her head. "It is unfortunate that he is so very handsome, however. A gentleman such as that, with a high title and excellent fortune would be a wonderful match for any young lady... if he had the character to go with it."

Unable to help herself, Louisa spoke up. "What has happened? Why is the Duke of Yarmouth now so ill considered by society?" She watched as her two sisters exchanged a glance, only for Rachel to turn her attention to her.

"Of course you would not have heard, I quite forgot that you do not join us when we attend balls and the like," she said, in a tone which was so utterly condescending, Louisa had to squeeze one of her hands into a tight fist so as not to let angry words escape her. "The Duke of Yarmouth has not been present in society for some months, though he was always very frequent in his visits to London before that. Last evening, he was speaking with Lady Wigton and her daughter, Lady Hannah, only for Lady Hannah to tell not only him but, given that she spoke loudly, also the rest of the *ton* about his actions towards her dear friend, Lady Sara."

"Lady Sara who is now Lady Huddersfield," Ruth broke in. "So she is married and contented. Thankfully, these rumours cannot tarnish her reputation now, though I do hope hat her husband knew of it all beforehand otherwise that might be rather difficult."

Louisa glanced from Ruth to Rachel and then back again. "What was it that the Duke did?" she asked, when her sisters did not continue speaking. "Is he something of a rascal?"

"More like a scoundrel, I would say!" Ruth clicked her tongue in obvious disapproval. "The gentleman is more than a little selfish, it seems, for he not only stole Lady Sara's affections by promising her that they would soon marry – though he begged her to keep their connection a secret with reasons that she went on to believe – he then went in search of other young ladies when he grew tired of her! Meanwhile, Lady Sara had turned away two other gentlemen who sought out her company, believing that the Duke of Yarmouth would soon propose and she would be wed."

"But he did not." Louisa frowned hard as her sisters shook their heads. "Lady Sara's heart must have been broken."

"Not only that, but she had turned away those two other gentlemen, making the *ton* believe that she had no interest in matrimony." Rachel sighed heavily. "She must have told all of this to Lady Hannah, given that they were dear friends. However, I do not think that the Duke himself ever expected news of his poor behaviour to escape to the *ton* for I heard that, when Lady Hannah threw those things towards him, he went very pale indeed."

Louisa's eyebrows lifted. "But he did not deny anything that was said?"

Both of her sisters shook their heads and Louisa closed her eyes briefly, both relieved and a little concerned. "You both must make certain to stay away from the Duke of Yarmouth. You cannot have him in your company and you certainly cannot ever have him here in the house. Do you understand me?"

Ruth let out a snort of laughter. "Why should the Duke of Yarmouth come here? He is not acquainted with any of us!"

"I am aware of that, but if he *should* become acquainted with you, I want you both to make certain that you do not linger in his company. It is very important indeed to protect your own reputations, especially since you are both seeking a match this Season."

Ever since their mother had passed away at the time of Ruth's birth, Louisa had been almost solely responsible for both of her sisters. With one older brother in line to take on the title and a father who, seemingly caring very little for his children, had thrown himself entirely into his business affairs, it had become Louisa's responsibility to make sure that both Rachel and Ruth were ready for society. There had been a governess, of course, but her father had seemingly decided that both an older sister and a governess were not required and, therefore, had dismissed the governess once Ruth had reached the appropriate age for her come out and left the rest on Louisa's shoulders. He had not seemed to be aware of her own need to seek out a match, had simply ignored that part of Louisa's life and instead, had instructed her to make certain that both of her sisters found excellent husbands. She was now considered their chaperone and all of society knew of it. In the same way, her own sisters did not seem to think about Louisa's desire for a husband, never once speaking of it or considering Louisa's own situation. To both of them, to her father and even to society, she was viewed as a spinster, even though she was not of age to be so. It was a great and heavy burden and one that Louisa was forced to continually carry alone – and at times, it almost felt too great to endure. Even now, as they spoke of the Duke, Louisa was forced to remind herself that her role was not to do anything for herself but instead, to guide and protect her sisters.

Even when they wed, I shall have no opportunity for matrimony, she thought to herself, sadness building in her heart. *I will be considered a spinster by then and what hope shall I have?*

A giggle caught her attention, pulling her from her own

considerations and she frowned, seeing Rachel quickly adjusting her expression so that she did not smile in even the smallest way.

"We have no intention of acquainting ourselves with the Duke of Yarmouth, I assure you." Rachel sighed and looked away, though there still remained a glimmer in her eyes. "Though I do wish that he was not so handsome. That would make it a little easier to ignore him."

A spark of interest flickered in Louisa's heart but she ignored it quickly, dismissing it as only a passing thought and nothing worth her attention. She was not about to let her thoughts linger on a gentleman of ignoble character, especially when she knew him to be nothing more than a scoundrel! It would be quite different if the *ton* were speaking of a man because of his charitable nature or because of his kindness towards those lesser than him, but to have them speak of his selfishness, inconsideration and general arrogance meant that he was someone they had all to avoid.

"I will point him out to you, if you wish it."

Louisa looked back at Ruth, seeing the slight flicker in her sister's eyes. "I hardly think that will be necessary."

"You were thinking of him, yes?"

"Yes, but not in the way that you think," Louisa answered, feeling heat begin to burn in her face though she kept her gaze steady all the same. "I was reflecting on the fact that such a gentleman ought not to be worth even a moment of our time, even if he *is* the most handsome and holds the highest title in all of society, save only for the King." With a slight clearing of her throat, she looked away from her sister. "Now, we should make certain that you are both thoroughly prepared for this evening. The new ballgowns have arrived, yes?"

"Yes, they have." Rachel tilted her head. "Including one for you. I did not know that you had purchased one."

Louisa blinked in surprise. "One for me?"

Her sister nodded, then frowned. "You did not purchase a ballgown, then? You seem to be rather astonished."

"I am, simply because I did *not* purchase a gown," Louisa answered, all the more confused. "I recall that we had gowns fitted for you both but I... " She trailed off as understanding overtook her. Her eyes closed and she let out a small sigh, though a smile edged up the corners of her mouth. "Julia. Of course."

When she opened her eyes, her two sisters were looking at each other, though Ruth, at least, smiled when she returned her gaze back to Louisa.

"Your friend is very considerate."

"Yes," Louisa agreed, thinking of Julia who had long been her friend and was, indeed, her closest friend. "How glad I am that she is in London with us at this time."

"You... you are not thinking about seeking out a match for yourself also, are you?" Rachel blinked quickly, her eyes widening just a little as she turned her gaze to Louisa and then returned it to Ruth, seemingly shocked at the idea that Louisa might herself be considering her future. "You know that father has given you a responsibility for us and -"

A rush of irritation had words snapping from Louisa's mouth in a manner which she would have never considerately spoken. The shock on Rachel's face as she thought about Louisa seeking out her own match as well as the touch of horror in her voice – as though it would be truly horrendous if Louisa were to do so – riled her in a way that filled her with a sense of deep frustration and upset.

"You are aware, Rachel, that I am also of eligible age, are you not?"

Rachel hesitated, then looked to Ruth again though her sister merely dropped her gaze to her hands.

"Yes, I am aware but I had always considered that *we* were to be your sole focus."

"And for what reason did you think that?" Louisa asked, finding herself on her feet, heat pouring from the tips of her toes to the top of her head. "Yes, father has given me this responsibility, as you have said, but it seems to me that both he *and* you have seemingly ignored – or forgotten – that I might have some hopes and desires for my own future! What will become of me when both Ruth and yourself find a match, Rachel? You will be happy and settled and contented, no doubt, but what of me?"

Rachel blinked quickly, then shrugged. "You will have a chance to then seek out your own match?"

It was as though something within Louisa broke, hearing her

sister's nonchalant remark, seeing the shrug of her shoulders. Her hands balled into fists, tears coming into her eyes. "I will be considered a spinster by then, Rachel! Do you not see that? Do you not *think* of that? Or is everything about this Season – about our *life* – entirely to do with you and your happiness?"

Silence flooded the room and suddenly, Louisa felt herself very ashamed of the explosion of feeling she had released upon her sisters. She saw them look at each other, saw the wide eyes and the slight paleness in Rachel's cheeks and felt her own anger fade significantly, leaving only mortification.

"At least Julia thinks of me," she muttered, making for the door rather than linger here with her two sisters and the tension she had now managed to create. "She is the one who purchased the ballgown for me for she knew that father had not permitted me to purchase one for myself."

"Wait, Louisa, please!" Ruth got to her feet, hurrying towards Louisa as she continued to make her way to the door. "We did not know that father had refused you such a thing. We thought that you simply did not need or want one."

Louisa closed her eyes and dropped her head, one hand on the door handle, the other hand now being grasped tightly by her sister. Rachel remained seated on the couch, however, not saying a single word.

"I have carried this burden for a long time, Ruth, and I ought not to have let myself speak with such inconsideration." Louisa offered her sister a small, rueful smile, aware of the ache in her heart. "Forgive me. I – I shall go and make certain that my own gown fits me quite properly, even though I will not be considered by any gentlemen this evening."

"Do not say that!" Ruth exclaimed, as Louisa opened the door, tugging her hand out of Ruth's gentle grasp. "I am sure that many a gentleman would look at you, Louisa. It may be that they simply do not know that you are seeking a match!"

Louisa shook her head, tears in her eyes now which she attempted to hold back, albeit without success. "I have a duty to Rachel and to yourself," she said, her voice nothing but a throaty whisper as she looked into her sister's face. "That must come first. Please, forget all that I have said. It... it does not matter, not really." Refusing to listen to her sister's gentle protests, Louisa stepped out of the door and closed it tightly behind her, ashamed of the way she had lost her composure. She had said more than she had ever intended to say, had railed at both of her sisters without thought or consideration and now, for whatever reason, the weight of her responsibility to them sat all the heavier on her shoulders.

The new ballgown would be wonderful to wear and was very kind indeed of Julia, but it would not take away from the fact that Louisa herself had no prospect of even standing up with a gentleman at the ball this evening. She was a chaperone and one day soon, would be a spinster... and nothing, it seemed, could prevent that.

Chapter Three

Joseph scowled. "Mother, I must insist that you desist!"

The Duchess ignored him, walking up and down the drawing room, wringing her hands.

"I am aware that this is not something that pleases you but it is done now. It cannot be taken back."

"This will quite ruin our family! Our reputation!" The Duchess closed her eyes tightly, standing still for a few moments as the shock of it all seemed to hit her all over again, even though it had been over a sennight since his unfortunate encounter with Lady Hannah. "Your brothers..."

"My brothers are wed and settled, so there is nothing to concern yourself with there," Joseph said firmly, attempting to pull his mother out of her upset and frustration. "You are behaving nonsensically."

"Nonsensically?" The Duchess whirled about on her heel, color flooding her cheeks. "I do not think that you understand what it is you have done! First of all, you ought to be ashamed of your treatment of Lady Sara for it is utterly despicable and, were she not already wed, I would insist that you marry her. Secondly," the Duchess continued, taking in a deep breath, "you should consider all that the *ton* is saying of you! You had something of a roguish reputation already, which concerned me, but now you are being called a scoundrel and a worthless man, which given your title and your family, is of great concern! However are you to marry if you continue to be spoken of in this way? If you continue to *behave* in this way?"

Closing his eyes, Joseph spread out his hands. "Mother, for the last few months, you have done everything in your power to make my life nothing short of miserable – and you have succeeded, I might add. You have found every way possible to frustrate and irritate me, going so far as to sell my most beloved pair of horses and stating that I had given you permission to do so! In my anger, I consented to coming to London to seek a bride and even though I have done as you asked, you still complain now about the whispers you find here about me." Despite the fact that he did not much like being called a reprobate with the very worst sort of character, Joseph had accepted it as a consequence of what he had done. His mother, however, simply could not. "Either you will determine to find me a bride regardless of this or you will leave me be and I will do just as I please in London." He lifted his chin a notch as his mother closed her eyes again and took in a shaking breath. "Now, I have no time to debate this further. I am going to attend Lord Wilson's ball and if you wish to join me, then might I suggest that you make your way to the carriage directly."

"And just how am I to find you a bride with all of these rumours?"

Joseph did not answer. Instead, he simply made his way directly from the drawing room, and down the staircase towards his carriage. Yes, he knew that those in society would be looking at him this evening, that there would be many a gloved hand hiding whispered words from their mouth but what could he do? This was something that he could not hide from and his pride told him that he certainly could *not* hide himself away! That would make things all the worse. Climbing into the carriage, he waited for a few moments and was about to raise his hand to rap on the roof, only for his mother to then appear at the door. She was handed in by a footman, though she scowled darkly.

"I do wish that you would show some remorse over this!" she exclaimed, as the carriage began to roll forward again. "Quite how I am to find someone willing to marry you, I do not know... but, despite my concerns, I am determined to try."

Joseph let out a low groan, not hiding it from his mother but making it quite plain that he had no desire for her to do such a thing. This, unfortunately, did not have the desired effect for she began to berate him all over again, right up until they reached the townhouse of Lord Wilson. Filled with frustration at his mother's harsh words and a sense of gnawing unease – which he did his best to ignore – Joseph climbed down from the carriage, lifted his head, set his shoulders and walked towards the house, leaving his mother behind. He had no interest in hearing anything more of what she had to say, no desire to allow her to drag him this way and that in the ballroom in the hope of finding a young lady to introduce him to. No, this evening, he might sink back into the shadows and hide himself away just a little, until the rumors and the whispers finally began to die down.

***

"Ouch!"

Turning, Joseph's elbow connected with something solid and another soft cry was heard. He stepped back, putting his hands to his waist, elbows out as a young lady rubbed at her side, a frown on her face as she held his gaze.

"You should be watching where you are going, sir," she said, curtly. "I would prefer you not to have stepped on my toes and then elbowed me in the side! You are not the only one here."

"So it seems." Joseph sniffed, then forced himself to incline his head though no words of apology came to his lips. "Though," he continued, finding himself a little irritated, "is it not a little unusual for a lady such as yourself to be standing back here... alone?" A sudden interest sparked in him as he took her in, seeing the light brown curls, the faint color in her cheeks and the soft blue eyes. Her gaze, however, quickly hardened as though she knew precisely what it was he was thinking, her stance growing a little stronger in the way she pulled back her shoulders and stood as straight as she could.

"I am chaperone to my sisters. They are both dancing this evening."

"Chaperone?" Joseph studied her again, thinking her a little young to have such a responsibility. "Then is your husband not present with you?"

A stiffness came into her frame, her eyes narrowing. "I am unwed."

Joseph's eyebrow lifted just as fresh color rushed into the lady's cheeks. "I see." He found himself smiling inwardly at the way this remark sent her gaze tumbling away from him, her hands clasping tightly in front of her. Clearly, his presence made her a little uncomfortable though, Joseph considered, it was not the first young lady who had felt that way and he had managed to conquer all of them thus far.

Might I be so bold as to try? It is not as though society is going to be willing to accept me, is it? So why should I not?

"Might I enquire as to your name?"

She threw him a look, her lip curling just a little. "If you wish to be introduced, then might I suggest you do so properly?"

"But I do not know anyone who is acquainted with you."

The lady closed her eyes, a heavy breath escaping from her. "In case I have not made myself plain, sir, I have no interest in being acquainted with a strange gentleman who has not only injured me but, thereafter, seeks to do whatever he can to disconcert me."

Joseph blinked in surprise, his smile fading.

"You did not truly believe that I have been entirely unaware of your intentions thus far, did you?" A note of mirth entered the lady's voice, making Joseph scowl. "Quite why any gentleman would wish to do such a thing, I cannot imagine, especially when he has caused pain and harm to a lady but, given that *you* have done so, I suppose that must only mean that you are not much of a gentleman!"

The shock of her boldness made Joseph's mouth drop open, astonishment flooding him. Never had he been spoken to in such a way by any young lady and yet this stranger, this blue-eyed young lady thought that she could do so with boldness and determination. It was so utterly shocking that Joseph did not know what to say, finding any sort of response fading from him as the lady let out a quiet laugh, shaking her head at his reaction.

"I do hope that my son has not been troubling you."

Joseph cleared his throat, trying to regain his composure as he turned his head to see his mother approaching, a light frown on her face. "Mother, please do not interject yourself into all my conversations. It is entirely unnecessary."

The only response to this, however, was a long, cold look and Joseph was forced, in the end, not only to pull his gaze away from her but to drop his head.

"Your son was just about to apologise for injuring me," the lady said, gesturing to Joseph as the Duchess caught her breath. "It was an accident, of course, for he did not see me here in the shadows."

Joseph inclined his head again, realizing that he had no choice now but to speak words of apology. "It was quite by accident, as you have said. Nonetheless, I deeply apologise for what occurred. I did not mean to injure you in the least. I was simply stepping back from society for a short time."

"Hiding, you mean." The irony in his mother's voice made Joseph scowl and he turned away from them both. "I should take my leave."

The thought of lingering here was not a pleasant one and despite the fact that he was a little concerned about what he might come up against as he made his way back through society, Joseph made his way into the middle of the room, trying to ignore the sidelong glances.

"I must say, old boy, if you do not remove that scowl from your face, you will never find any young ladies to consider you!"

Joseph turned sharply, about to make a sharp retort in return, only for his face to split with a smile, his spirits lifting instantly. "Quillon! Whatever are you doing here? When did you return from the Great Adventure?"

His friend – someone who had long been his *closest* friend before he had decided to take his leave of England and travel through foreign lands in the hope of excitement and adventure – grinned broadly. "Did you not hear? I became dreadfully ill in France and had to return home to recuperate!"

"You did?" Joseph's smile fell away as his friend nodded. "No, I did not hear. I thought you might have written but –"

"I was much too weak, I am afraid." A sudden somberness came over the Marquess of Quillon's expression. "It was a rather dangerous, difficult time but I am recovered now, as you can see." He grinned again, a lightness returning to his voice. "And my first thought was to come to London, to delight myself with society again and find myself happy. It has been some time since I was not free of fear or the like. I was sure that I would find you here also, though I must say, I have heard some rumours about you which I found a little... surprising?"

Joseph winced. "A lot has happened since you went off on your Great Adventure. You were gone for nearly two years now, were you not?"

"I was."

Lifting his shoulders in a shrug, Joseph tried to dismiss the stab of embarrassment which pierced his heart at the thought of informing his friend that the rumors he had heard were, unfortunately, true.

"You were always something of a rascal but I did not think you would ever become a rogue."

Joseph rolled his eyes and pushed aside all thought of embarrassment. "Please tell me that you have not come to London in order to berate me?" he said, pushing a note of humor into his voice. "I have already got my mother here and she is both ashamed of me and vocal with it! I do not think I can take any more criticism."

His friend tilted his head, studying Joseph for a moment before, with a shrug, he nodded. "Very well, we will not speak of what I have heard, nor the rumours that you have pulled to yourself." Turning, he spread one arm out wide towards the ballroom. "Do you intend to dance this evening? Shall we wait here to see which young ladies might be *bold* enough to come and speak with you so you might, thereafter ask them to dance? Or have you had enough of the *ton*'s attention for the evening?"

"The latter, I assure you," Joseph muttered, catching yet another lady giving him the cut direct as she made her way past. "The card room, mayhap?"

Lord Quillon grinned. "Capital. Come then, you lead the way."

Chapter Four

"Might I enquire as to your name?"

Louisa resisted the urge to rub her side, disliking the gentleman intensely. Thus far, he had not only been incredibly rude towards her but she could practically see the thoughts that were running through his mind. He was clearly trying to make her feel a little uncertain, to set her off-balance simply because she had had the audacity to demand an apology from him and had stated outright that his behavior was entirely improper. He was rather handsome with a shock of dark hair and clear, green eyes but the smile on his lips was not a pleasant one and his remarks towards her had been most improper. Clearly, he wanted her to feel ill at ease.

But I am not about to be so. She did not know his name nor his title but there was certainly nothing about him that made her want to be introduced to him! "If you wish to be introduced, then might I suggest you do so properly?"

A hint of a smirk touched the edge of the gentleman's lips. "But I do not know anyone who is acquainted with you."

Louisa let out a slow breath, feeling that stir of frustration in her chest which she was determined not to reveal to him. Her eyes closed briefly as she strengthened herself, then looked back at him. "In case I have not made myself plain, sir, I have no interest in being acquainted with a strange gentleman who has not only injured me but, thereafter, seeks to do whatever he can to disconcert me." Seeing his smile begin to fade, she let her own lips quirk. "You did not truly believe that I have been entirely unaware of your intentions thus far, did you?" Seeing him begin to frown, she let laughter enter her voice, doing so quite deliberately so that he would see she was not about to give in to all that had been said. "Quite why any gentleman would wish to do such a thing, I cannot imagine, especially when he has caused pain and harm to a lady but, given that *you* have done so, I suppose that must only mean that you are not much of a gentleman!"

The shock that leapt into his face made her laugh – properly this time – though this seemed to astonish him all the more. His mouth dropped open, his eyes rounding.

"I do hope that my son has not been troubling you."

Louisa's gaze pulled from the gentleman towards a lady who came to join them, her sharp eyes going to the gentleman before returning to Louisa, a question in her expression.

The gentleman, however, cleared his throat, his mouth pulling into a flat line. "Mother, please do not interject yourself into all my conversations. It is entirely unnecessary."

The ice which the lady sent towards her son made Louisa's eyebrows lift. Whoever this was, it was clear to her that he had no great standing in her eyes and that, she considered, said a good deal about his character. When the lady returned her gaze to Louisa, she offered a brief smile and then gestured to him. "Your son was just about to apologise for injuring me. It was an accident, of course, for he did not see me here in the shadows." Her eyebrows lifted gently as she looked back to the gentleman, fully aware that, as yet, he had not apologized and relishing the opportunity to force those words from his lips. Thankfully, he did not disappoint her for he spoke quickly, inclining his head again.

"It was quite by accident, as you have said. Nonetheless, I deeply apologise for what occurred. I did not mean to injure you in the least. I was simply stepping back from society for a short time."

"Hiding, you mean."

The way that the lady spoke with such vehemence made Louisa start in surprise, a little taken aback. She could find nothing to say, only for the gentleman then to incline his head towards his mother, refusing to look at Louisa again.

"I should take my leave."

Louisa could only watch as the gentleman walked away quickly, apparently very unwilling to linger. Given what his mother had said to him and the manner in which she had said it, Louisa could understand him though she did not feel in the least bit sorry for him.

"I am truly sorry for whatever it was the Duke did that injured you."

Astonishment ricocheted up through Louisa's frame. "The Duke?"

The lady nodded and Louisa quickly dropped into a curtsy, realizing the standing of the lady before her. "Your Grace, I did not know –"

"Please." Reaching out, the lady grasped Louisa's hand and pressed it. "You need not show such deference, especially when my son has treated you so ill! I must say, however, I was rather impressed with how you spoke with him."

All the more astonished, Louisa blinked rapidly as her heart thudded. "You overheard me speaking to him?"

"I did. I did not move forward to join you until my frustration grew to such heights, I could no longer contain myself." A flickering smile crossed her face, though it held no joy. "The Duke of Yarmouth is not a name which commands respect, not any longer. Though I must say, I did not think that anyone would have the strength of character to speak to him in the way that you did. It was most refreshing." Eyeing her carefully – though Louisa simply stood there in silence, not sure what to say – the Duchess' lips curved into a smile. "Might I ask your name? I realise that we have not been formally acquainted but I should very much like to know you."

"But of course." The protest that Louisa had made previously to the Duke about the lack of acquaintance did not even ring in her mind as she curtsied properly. "Lady Louisa, Your Grace. My father is the Earl of Jedburgh." When she lifted her gaze, she caught the flicker of recognition in the Duchess' eyes. "It is very pleasant to make your acquaintance, of course."

"I knew your mother, God rest her," the Duchess answered, softly. "She and I were in London together, making our debut. She married your father and I married my dear husband. I was very sorry to hear of her passing though I understand that was a long time ago now."

Louisa nodded, a lump coming into her throat though she pushed it away quickly. "My sister, Ruth, was only a baby at a time. Now, however, she is making her debut."

"I see." The Duchess tilted her head, still studying Louisa. "Might I ask, then, where your father is?"

Heat poured into Louisa's face as she realized what the lady meant. She herself was standing alone, without a chaperone and without her father nearby. Did the Duchess think her improper? Did she believe that there was some reason for Louisa's presence here, that she might be hoping for a secret liaison with another gentleman? "My father is in the card room, I expect," she said, quickly. "I am responsible for and chaperone to my sisters. They are both dancing at present, one with Lord Proudfoot and the other with Lord Sibminster."

The Duchess frowned. "But you are of age to wed, are you not?"

A little unsure as to how to respond, for she did not know the lady well and yet could not simply refuse to answer the Duchess' probing questions, Louisa spread out her hands. "It is a responsibility that I have been given." Her hands fell back to her sides as she looked away again, finding the Duchess' examining gaze to be rather intense. "Mayhap, when they both make a good match, I might then have an opportunity."

The Duchess said nothing, though she nodded slowly as if to agree with Louisa that this might well be the case. Louisa licked her lips and kept her gaze turned away from the lady, a little confused as to what the Duchess had meant by such a question and wondering what it was that she was thinking.

"That must be a little trying for you, my dear." There was kindness in the Duchess' voice and Louisa, looking at her again, felt tears begin to build behind her eyes though she held them back with force. "I do wonder if... well, that does not matter. Your father is the Earl of Jedburgh, you say?"

"Yes, that is so." Louisa wanted to ask more, wanted to understand what it was that she meant by such questions but instead, was forced to keep them back as her two sisters were brought back to join her by the gentlemen they had been dancing with. Louisa quickly introduced them both to the Duchess and, much to her relief, both of her sisters responded with due deference just as they ought. Soon, the Duchess took her leave of them all, though not before she sent another quick look towards Louisa, a look which held a good many questions – though Louisa did not know as to what.

"There you are! I have been looking all over for you!"

All of Louisa's questions over the Duchess faded in a

moment as she beamed at Lady Julia before twirling around, showing off the gown that her friend had purchased for her.

"I knew that this was your doing," she said, as Lady Julia grinned, her brown eyes twinkling. "You did not need to do so, however. You know that there is no need for me to wear a gown and prance around the room!"

"Now, now, there is no reason why you should not look your very best," Lady Julia answered, throwing a look to Rachel and to Ruth, both of whom quickly dropped their gaze, a hint of shame coming into each of their expressions. "I think that you ought to be treated just as well as your sisters and, if your father does not care to do so, then I shall."

Louisa took her friend's hand and squeezed it. "You are very kind. You cannot know of how happy it made me to know I should be wearing something so beautiful."

Lady Julia's expression softened. "It was my pleasure. My father and mother do not care how many gowns I purchase and it was a joy to be able to do so for you." She linked arms with Louisa as she, Ruth and Rachel all began to meander back towards the center of the ballroom where, no doubt, the next two gentlemen that were to dance with her sisters would soon come to find them.

"You must tell me what the Duchess of Yarmouth was doing speaking with you," Lady Julia said as Louisa shrugged lightly. "She appeared to be most intense in her conversation and in her manner! I saw you speaking with her, you see, and I did not want to interrupt so I stood to the side for a time."

"Her son not only stepped on my foot but also thrust an elbow into my side," Louisa answered, with a wry smile. "She appeared to make certain all was well. Thereafter, she asked about my father and my title and that is all that took place, really."

Lady Julia's eyes narrowed though not in an unfriendly way. "She asked about your father?"

"Well, you must admit, it must have appeared a little strange to her to see me standing in the shadows, alone! I had to explain that I am chaperone to my sisters –"

"Something which should never have been put in place."

"And that I have no time to consider matrimony for myself," Louisa continued, ignoring the remark even though she knew her friend was correct in her thinking. "She did ask about my father twice, however, as though she wanted to remember his name. I do not know why."

Lady Julia frowned, her lips pressing flat together for a moment or two. "I do not know either. I have heard that the Duchess of Yarmouth is a very kind, considerate lady. Her interest is not something that I would fear, if you understand what I mean."

Louisa nodded. "I do."

"It must be very difficult indeed to have such a son, however," Lady Julia continued, her expression twisting for a moment. "To know that the Duke is not only a scoundrel but also lacking any sort of regret for his behaviour is not only shocking but troubling too."

Recalling the exchange between the Duke and herself, Louisa let out a small, dry laugh. "He did not speak well to me, certainly. Neither did he show any sort of care or consideration. In fact, I would say that he behaved just as I might have expected him to, given all that I have heard of him." She gestured to her sisters, who were now making their way back towards the dance floor, each on the arm of a gentleman. "I have warned Ruth and Rachel to stay away from the Duke of Yarmouth and, now that I have spoken with him myself, I am all the more determined that they should do so!"

Her friend nodded. "I quite agree."

Louisa offered her a smile. "I hope that my conversation with the Duke was not only my first but will also be my last," she said, with determination. "In fact, I am telling you here and now that I will make every effort to make certain that it is so!"

Lady Julia chuckled softly. "A very fine decision, my dear friend." She patted Louisa's arm gently. "Let us hope that you succeed."

Chapter Five

"I have decided on a wife for you!"

Joseph let out a low groan and pinched the bridge of his nose lightly, telling himself that it was either a dream he was having, hearing the voice of his mother speaking so, or he was still addled from the amount of liquor he had imbibed the previous evening.

Unfortunately for him, neither of those things proved to be correct.

"Are you listening to me?" His mother strode towards Joseph, coming around the side of the dining room table and pulling out a chair so she might sit directly beside him. Her gaze was piercing and Joseph closed his eyes, pain shooting through his head.

"Mother, I am not in the mood to hear any such nonsense," he said with a low groan, though this did nothing whatsoever to convince her to remove herself from his company. "Please, I –"

"Will you listen to me and stop your fussing?" The Duchess tapped his arm lightly, then, as Joseph opened his eyes, signaled to the footman to pour him another coffee while she herself reached to pour the tea. "Now, you know as well as I that I have determined to find you a bride. I –"

"Yes, you have made that very clear over the last few months." Joseph scowled, though his mother scowled back at him, clearly frustrated at the interruption. "You have brought up the subject almost every day."

She sniffed. "In fact, I believe I have mentioned it every single day," she replied, her tone laced with sarcasm. "Now, I will admit that when I heard what Lady Hannah said of you and when I saw the rumours and whispers that would follow, I feared that my task would fail utterly and you would triumph."

Joseph rolled his eyes. "This is not a contest between us, Mother."

"Oh yes, it is." Taking a sip of her tea, she let the silence challenge him for a few moments before she continued again – and in the quiet, Joseph could find nothing to say. It seemed that, whatever he said, she was ready with an answer. Frustrated, he gripped his hands tight together under the table, his jaw jutting forward but his mother took no notice.

"There will be no young ladies willing to turn towards you," she stated, her tone crisp and her words short. "Or even if there were, their mothers or fathers would not permit them – and this, despite your title and your standing! You know why they will not even consider you. It is shameful to me and it ought to be to you also."

"Please." Joseph let out a long, exasperated sigh, quite certain that this tirade – and the supposed decision as regards his bride to be – would be nothing but nonsense. This was taking far too long and given the pain in his head, he did not have much time for her long, drawn out explanations that would lead to either another argument between them or silence from him as he steadfastly refused to do as she suggested.

"You wish me to get to the point. Very well." Rather than speaking, however, his mother took another sip of her tea and then, settling the cup back in the saucer, turned to look directly at him. "Yarmouth, I have decided to approach the Earl of Jedburgh."

This meant nothing to Joseph and, from his blank stare towards her, he presumed that his mother recognized this given the way she sighed.

"He has three daughters," she continued, after a moment, letting out a huff of breath in obvious frustration. "I am sure that one of them could be... encouraged to consider you."

Joseph rolled his eyes, not caring in the least that his mother saw him. "You have already told me that you do not think that any mother or father of any young lady would be willing to push them towards me. What makes you think that this Lord Jedburgh will be any different?"

A glimmering smile crossed his mother's face and Joseph frowned, not liking it in the least.

"This is a different situation."

"Why?" Joseph's eyes narrowed a little as his mother opened her mouth and then closed it again with a snap, shaking her head. "Mother, you must inform me as to why this young lady's father would be willing to offer her hand to me. Is she very plain? Is that what your punishment is to be?"

At this, the Duchess' lips thinned and her shoulders lifted just a little. "There are times that I forget just how shallow you are in your thoughts and your considerations, only for you to then remind me of them with great force."

Her words stung but Joseph did not so much as flinch, looking back at her with a steady gaze as he fought to ascertain what it was about this lady that would make her father willing to consent. "She must be a wallflower, then. Or disgraced herself!"

"I can assure you that she is not." The Duchess drew herself up as best she could in her chair. "There is nothing but respectability about the lady and I will not have you suggest otherwise."

A sudden concern began to flood though Joseph's heart as he watched the confidence grow in his mother's expression. The small smile had returned to her lips, a glint in her eye that could not be taken as anything other than a certainty of her success. Surely it could not be? Surely it would be that his mother's attempts would be thwarted due to the rumors about him? Yes, it had not been pleasant to have Lady Hannah say such things to him and it had been all the worse to know that the *ton* now considered him a scoundrel but there had been some good in it – that being that his mother would no longer be able to force a bride upon him.

Perhaps, he considered, his confidence in *that* had been a little too strong. The way that she was looking at him told him that there was more to this than he had first thought.

"What is wrong with the lady that her father will willingly offer her hand to me, a gentleman known to be a scoundrel and a rogue?" he asked, speaking plainly as his mother flinched visibly, still injured by what society now thought of him. "If she is not disgraced herself, is it that she has been already wed? Is she divorced?" The latter suggestion made sense to him, for a divorced lady was ill considered by society and none would look upon her again, even though it would have been her husband who would have forced that situation upon her. "I will not marry a divorced lady."

"For heaven's sake, Yarmouth, must you be so very

particular?" His mother threw up her hands and, gripping the edge of the table thereafter, rose so sharply that her chair scraped back across the floor. "You have only just informed me about all that the things that the *ton* thinks of you and yet, somehow, you have a difficulty in even the thought of attaching yourself to a lady who might herself have some of the very same issues as you!"

Seeing the double standard his mother held out to him did not change Joseph's thoughts in any way. "I will not wed a disgraced nor a divorced lady."

She shook her head at him. "It is just as well that she is neither of those things, then," she answered, stoutly. "Now, as I have said, I will go to speak with the Earl of Jedburgh and –"

"Wait." Urgency and dread spiraled together and, before he knew it, Joseph was out of his seat, though he stood at the table rather than coming after his mother. "You cannot simply go to a gentleman on my behalf! I am a Duke in my own right! To have my mother pursuing a match for me is not only laughable, it is mortifying."

"And yet, that is what I shall do."

Joseph closed his eyes, telling himself that he ought to have expected that sort of response.

"You already agreed to this," she reminded him, as the footman opened the door for her. "You agreed to my finding you a match this Season, do you not recall?"

"Only because you were a relentless tormentor, unyielding in your torment," he muttered darkly, running a hand through his hair, the onset of a throbbing headache intensifying as he squeezed his eyes shut, striving to combat the wave of anxiety that threatened to engulf him. "After everything that has happened, I do not think that –"

"I will inform you about what takes place," she interrupted, giving him another quick glance before sailing out of the door. Joseph, his mouth still half-open given that he had not quite finished what it was he wanted to say, watched her leave, feeling his panic begin to grow all the more. When his mother had first entered the dining room and informed him of her intentions, he had quickly dismissed it as something that could quickly be dismissed. Now, however, he was not so sure.

Swallowing hard, he sank back down into his seat and then closed his eyes, breathing hard as he attempted to regain control of his emotions.

"She cannot force me to marry anyone," he told himself aloud, thumping one fist on the table. "She might force an engagement, she might even force me to the church but she cannot *ever* force me to say, 'I do'."

***

"I am glad to see you." Joseph walked alongside his friend through the heart of London, letting his gaze flick from side to side as he took in the expressions of those who passed him, seeing how some looked at him with interest whilst others quickly looked away, as though horrified to have even seen him with their own eyes. "You must tell me all about your Great Adventure."

"Must I?" Lord Quillon chuckled, then shrugged. "I have a good many stories I can share, yes, but I must tell you that I have no intention of lingering on the difficulties that I endured." He winced. "They were very difficult days indeed and, at times, I was not certain I would survive, given how weak I became."

Joseph's eyes widened as he stopped walking and looked directly back at his friend. "You did not inform me of this. Had I known, I would have given up everything and come to your aid."

"I was too weak to write – or even to inform one of my servants to write to you – and when I began to recover, I did not see that there was any great need." Lord Quillon smiled, though there was no light in his eyes and Joseph realized, with a heaviness settling on his heart, just how much his friend had endured. "I have returned to London with a fresh perspective on life, however."

Joseph began to walk again, glancing across at Lord Quillon. "Oh?"

"I have decided to take a wife. I think it is high time that I do so, given that I have a good many responsibilities and no-one under me who could take on the title, should I go onto the next life."

A slight shudder ran through Joseph's frame as he took in Lord Quillon's words. "But you survived, you endured! You need not fear your passing now."

"No, but who is to say when it may come?" Lord Quillon's shoulders lifted and then fell. "I may fall ill with another severity and, given that I am still a little weak, I may not survive it! Therefore, I have decided not only to take a wife but also to make certain that I have the heir produced within the year."

Joseph tried to smile, keeping his tone light as he fought back against the severity which had hit him. "What if it is a daughter?"

Lord Quillon chuckled. "Then I shall try again and again until I manage to produce the heir! Otherwise, the line will fall to my wastrel cousin and I do not want that."

Nodding in understanding, Joseph considered his own brothers. They were both far more responsible and considered than him. "I do not have that same concern, I must say."

"Because of your brothers." A slightly dry tone hit Lord Quillon's voice. "Is that not a little… inconsiderate of your own responsibilities? You are simply leaving them to your brothers rather than taking them on yourself."

Joseph shook his head. "I have no interest in marrying. When I do – and I have already promised that I shall – I will do so in order to produce the heir and nothing more."

"Though you have no intention of marrying soon."

Wincing, Joseph looked away from his friend, turning his head so that he looked in the opposite direction. He did not want to speak of this, did not want to give it credence and yet it was a burden that, ever since his mother had spoken to him earlier that afternoon, now hung heavier around his shoulders. "My mother has insisted on finding me a match this Season."

Silence came from his friend and slowly, Joseph turned his attention back towards him, seeing the shock written across his friend's expression.

"She will not succeed, of course."

Lord Quillon cleared his throat gruffly, clearly trying to remove the surprise from his face. "Your mother is organising a match for you? Why do you not do it yourself?"

"Because I have no wish to marry, as I am sure I have just said!" Joseph let out a frustrated breath. "You do not know what I have endured, Quillon."

"Then tell me."

With a nod, Joseph rubbed one hand over his chin as they continued through the busy London street. "Some months ago, my mother informed me that it was high time I found a wife. We argued, I insisted that I be left alone and she determined to make my life nothing short of a misery – so she put it – until I relented and permitted her to do as she wished."

"Oh." Lord Quillon's voice had become very grave. "And might I surmise that she did as she had threatened?"

Joseph dropped his hand to his side and let out a low groan. "I cannot describe it to you. It was a difficulty rising from my bed at the end of it, knowing that I would face her at the dining room table. She spoke about marriage and my responsibilities for seemingly hours on end, almost constantly in my company and even when I was in my study at business matters, she would not relent – and I could not remove her! Adding to this, she then made herself a nuisance, making sure that the housekeeper served me meals I had not asked her to provide, refusing invitations and visitors before I could even see them and, what is worse, selling my most beloved pair of horses from under my very nose!"

Lord Quillon let out a low whistle.

"Precisely," Joseph muttered, shaking his head. "I thought I knew my mother well. Now, however, I see that she is cunning, determined and quite forceful in it! I could not endure any longer and thus, weakened by her constant haranguing, I relented."

"I see." His friend let out a sigh. "That is unfortunate. Though, now that you have had such rumours spoken of you, are you sure that she will be able to do as she has threatened? Is that what you meant by stating that she will not succeed?"

Joseph nodded. "Those rumours are dire, of course, though I will not pretend that I had nothing to do with them. However, I presume that with society turning away from me as it has, it is not as though any young lady is going to be eager to step towards me! My own mother told me that any sensible father or mother would not even *think* of permitting their daughter to come near me!"

"And yet, she thinks that she will be able to provide you with a wife?"

A knot of worry tied itself in Joseph's stomach. "I am afraid that she is clear in her determination. To add to this, she spoke to me earlier today about going to call upon Lord Jedburgh, in order to convince him that one of *his* daughters might be a suitable match."

"Lord Jedburgh? The Earl?"

Joseph stopped sharply. "Are you acquainted with him? Do you know his daughters?"

"I do, yes, though I cannot recall their names." Lord Quillon's expression grew thoughtful. "I believe that their mother passed away when they were all rather young. That is a pity."

Joseph barely listened to this, grasping a hold of his friend's arm in a sudden determination. "Are any of them very plain? Or a wallflower? Or disgraced in some way?"

A line formed between Lord Quillon's eyebrows, his gaze sharpening just a little. "Why do you ask such a thing?"

"Because I cannot see why else a father would consent to his daughter marrying someone with the reputation I have otherwise," Joseph explained, as his friend nodded slowly, rubbing one hand over his chin for a moment. "You have heard enough, I am sure, to make it quite clear to you that I cannot be considered by any of the *ton* as an acceptable match. Therefore, whoever this young lady is, there must be some defect in her or in her character which would, thereafter, force her father to attach himself to the idea with relish!"

Lord Quillon began to walk again. "From what I remember, none of the young ladies are particularly plain, they have not been disgraced and the family name is highly respectable. I would not think that there is anything about any of them that ought to concern you." He threw Joseph a glance. "Though I must say, it is a little surprising to hear you have such concerns when your own reputation is less than pristine!"

Joseph threw off the remark with a shrug. "There must be some reason as to why they would accept me. I just do not know what it is!"

"You are concerned." His friend's eyebrows lifted. "You think that she will be able to force your hand in that regard?"

Closing his eyes for a moment, Joseph let out a long, slow

breath. "In giving in to her, I have effectively given my consent." Shaking his head, Joseph opened his eyes and looked into his friend's face, seeing the frown lingering there. "And in my very heart, I fear that she might succeed."

Chapter Six

Louisa picked up her embroidery thread and prepared to continue on with the piece she had been working on for the last few weeks. While she did enjoy embroidery, it often gave her a little too much time to ruminate and that was proving to be a little... dissatisfying at the present moment.

"There is much for me to be thankful for," she told herself, firmly, as she threaded it through and then pulled it gently. "And I may still get my chance to wed one day."

That made her shoulders slump despite her positive words. She did not truly believe it, she realized, not when she knew just how long it might take for her sisters to wed. The *ton* would soon consider her a spinster and then what was she to do? She would be put on the shelf, no longer a viable match for any gentleman and her future, thereafter, would look rather bleak. Louisa could only hope that her father would be kind to her, that he himself would make certain that her future was secure so that she would not either have to find work as a governess or a nurse or depend on her sisters for lodging and food. Tears began to burn but Louisa blinked them away as quickly as she could, refusing to let them fall. Yes, her father had never really considered her but there was no sense in complaining about it, not when she knew nothing would change. She recalled the times she had attempted to ask her father about her own future and the fact that she might soon be considered a spinster, only for him to dismiss her outright. He had come down heavily upon her with his words, insisting that she put her responsibilities to her sisters first given that their mother was no longer with them. That had stirred Louisa's own guilt and she had decided thereafter never to bring it to her father again.

"So there can be no good in complaining about my situation to anyone, then, can there?" she murmured aloud, her voice echoing around the room. Her two sisters were still preparing for afternoon calls and very soon, Louisa expected, they would come to join her. Her smile lifted in a slightly rueful consideration as her thoughts went to the Duke of Yarmouth. So long as *he* did not call, then all would be well! Just as she was thinking on this, the door opened and, much to her surprise, her father strode into the room. He did not turn about and remove himself again when he saw her sitting there as she might have expected, however, for he was a gentleman who did not often like the company of his daughters. Instead, he sat down opposite her and, leaning forward, put his elbows on his knees and clasped his hands just under his chin. His eyes were piercing and Louisa set her embroidery aside at once, feeling a little concerned as to what this might mean. Her father had barely said more than a few sentences to her at any one point ever since their arrival in London so why was he now sitting opposite her with such a grave expression on his face? Had she failed him in some way?

"Father?" Louisa ventured, her voice wobbling a little. "Is there something the matter?"

The Earl of Jedburgh's eyebrows drifted low over his eyebrows, his mouth pulling flat as he looked away. He did not say anything for some moments, his dark hair seeming to cast a shadow across his features. Louisa's stomach began to twist, her whole body tightening with tension as her mind whirled with worry.

"Louisa." Eventually, he spoke though his tone remained heavy. "I have come to an agreement for your marriage."

Louisa blinked furiously, one hand gripping to the arm of the couch tightly as she stared back at her father.

"Your engagement will be announced within a sennight, once all the various agreements and the like have been made," the Earl continued as though all that he had said was nothing more than a minor conversation which would have very little effect upon Louisa herself. "However, I have said to the lady that I was concerned about my other two daughters, given that your responsibility is to them and she has agreed that the wedding will take place near the end of the Season, to give you as much time as possible in order for you to make certain that they make a good match. Though, given your connection, that will be a good deal easier, I think!" A glimmer of a smile touched the edges of his lips though it faded just as quickly. "Though, if neither of them make a match then your responsibility will continue for them into the next

Season also. This has been agreed between the lady and myself and I presume that you will have no objection?"

Louisa felt as though she had been taken out to sea and was now being hit and crushed by every wave, struggling to find her breath as she battled confusion. Her father's eyebrow lifted in question but still, Louisa could not speak. Never had she imagined that she would be offered such a thing as this, never had she thought that her father would take care of her future in such a way! It was not something that she had thought him interested in and yet, somehow, he had taken it upon himself to find her a suitable match! Yes, her responsibilities to her sisters had to continue but that was something that Louisa was more than willing to do. Her heart began to calm itself as a faint happiness began to warm through her. She was going to be wed! She might be able to have a family of her own, would be mistress of her own estate! Her happiness quickly faded as her mind began then to fill with all manner of questions, wondering who it was that her father had tied her to – and without even speaking to her about it first.

"You say that I am to marry?" she asked, her voice hoarse as her father nodded. Louisa closed her eyes, suddenly fearful that her father had found her an old, decrepit fellow who needed a wife to produce the heir for him before he passed. "I do not understand. You… you have never mentioned such a thing before and, indeed, told me that my sole responsibility was to my sisters. Once *they* wed, then I might have my opportunity, if I was still of eligible age."

Something passed across the Earl's face, something that Louisa could not quite make out. He looked away, clearing his throat gruffly as he rubbed one hand over his chin. "Yes, I am aware of my previous remarks on the subject."

Shame? Louisa frowned. *Could it be that my father has had a change of heart? That he now feels ashamed of his neglect of my future?*

"The lady made it quite clear as regards *her* thoughts as to the present situation and though I will not say that I was pleased by it – or that I was convinced – what she offered made my thoughts on your future change. I did suggest that one of my other daughters might suit, given that I am eager to see them wed but –"

"Why are you not eager to see *me* wed, Father?" Louisa found herself on her feet, a sudden anger coursing through her which appeared to knock her father back, given how he not only reared back but leaned back against the cushions of his seat. "What is it about my sisters that makes them of much more importance than me?"

The Earl blinked at her, his face paling a little. He then closed his eyes and heaved a sigh, though Louisa remained where she was, her hands now on her hips, her whole body tense with an anger at the injustice of how she had been treated for so long.

"It was your mother." Another heavy breath escaped him as the Earl rubbed one hand over his face. "She insisted that I make certain the girls were cared for, telling me that you would be my aid and my support."

Some of Louisa's anger faded. "But that does not mean that she thought I would not marry," she answered as her father turned a sorrowful gaze to her. "Do you not think that I would be just as caring and considered of my sisters and their unwed state even if I had the chance to marry?"

"That is... that is not what my thinking was," he admitted, a little hoarse now himself. "I always believed that... well, that she wanted the younger two girls to marry first."

Louisa's throat constricted. "I do not believe that my mother would have ever pushed me aside in favor of the other two," she said, tightly. "Can you not see that I would always have done my best for them? If I were to marry, then I would have an ever greater chance of succeeding in finding them a suitable match."

"Ah, but only if you married well." The Earl waggled one finger at her. "And there would also be the honeymoon and that can last well over a year! I could not permit that to happen. They need you as their chaperone, to guide them through society."

Closing her eyes against a fresh rush of angry tears, Louisa let her hands drop to her sides. "They have a father for that." Her voice was quiet, a little louder than a whisper and Louisa opened her eyes to see her father look away, his jaw tightening. Clearly, that suggestion had not been a good one. Whether it was mere selfishness on her father's part or something that, as yet, he had not told her about, it was clear that he had no interest in doing anything by way of responsibility for either Ruth's or Rachel's futures. That was still to remain on her shoulders.

"You will not have a honeymoon until your two sisters are married," the Earl told her, changing the subject completely and returning it back to Louisa's new engagement. "That was agreed with the lady and –"

"Who is this lady that you speak of?" Louisa asked, sitting back down, her shoulders heavy and her spirits low given the way her father had refused to take on any sort of responsibility for his daughters. "I do not understand what has taken place. Nor have you told me who it is that I am to marry."

Her father turned his full attention back towards her. "I believe that you are already acquainted with the Duchess of Yarmouth, yes?"

Louisa's breath caught in her chest, shock rippling through her as her father's eyebrow lifted in question. Surely it could not be that her father thought to marry her to the Duke of Yarmouth?

"I can see from your expression that yes, you are acquainted with her. I did not know of this so her arrival at the house this afternoon was rather surprising." The Earl cleared his throat again, perhaps aware that this next part of his conversation with her was not about to be a pleasant one. "She thinks that you will be an excellent match for her son. I believe that he has already consented."

Louisa could not breathe. She put one hand to her heart, feeling as though someone had come from behind and was squeezing her throat, hard. How could her father think to do this? What made him believe that marrying a gentleman with such a roguish character would be a good thing for her?

"Louisa?"

"I – I would rather remain unwed and a spinster than marry him," she wheezed, her chest heaving furiously as she finally managed to take in a breath. "Have you not heard of him, father? Have you not heard of what he has done?"

"I have. And yet, I believe that, given what the Duchess said, you will make a good wife for him."

"But he will not be a good husband for me!" Louisa cried, tears beginning to fall to her cheeks, her whole body screaming with an inexpressible pain. "I will be left with a gentleman who does what he pleases with whomever he pleases, while I remain at home, left to wonder what rumours will be swirling about him soon. Is that what you think I will be contented with?"

Her father shrugged, sniffing lightly as he rose from his chair. "Given what the Duchess said of you, I am sure that what you fear will not come to pass. You will have her as your companion and as your guide. She seemed to believe that her son can reform himself, only that he needs the right young lady to come alongside him."

"And she thinks that I am that lady?" Louisa laughed derisively, tears still falling to her cheeks. "She and I had one conversation, Father, *one*! She does not know my character in the least!"

"It is has been decided, Louisa."

Louisa's hands curled into tight fists as she attempted to control her tears, sobs still threatening to overtake her. "Father, please." Her words were filled with desperation, her heart pounding as fear poured into her veins. "You cannot force me to marry him."

Her father made his way to the door, his duty done. "You complained to me that you had no chance to marry, Louisa. Only just now, in this conversation, you stated that I was deeply wrong in making certain that only my younger two daughters found suitable matches rather than including you. Yet now that I give you a husband, now that I find you a match with a gentleman far above you in both title and wealth, you are not contented!" Putting one hand to the doorhandle, he pulled it open but did not step through it, turning his head to look at her, his gaze steady. "I can understand your concern but I am sure it will not be as dreadful as you think. To be wed to a Duke is an excellent thing, for your standing will improve and your sisters' chances of a good match will also increase. You will have the security you told me that you required for your future and I will have my responsibility to your mother fulfilled. I cannot see what your concern is."

Louisa flung herself out of her chair but her legs were so weak, she could only take a few tottering steps forward. "But no-one will want to be connected with our family, not when they know that I am engaged to a rogue!"

The Earl let out a snort as though he did not know what it was she was talking about. "My dear girl, are you so foolish as to believe that? The Duke of Yarmouth may be a scoundrel, yes, but to be connected to a Duke in some way is still seen as an excellent thing. I can assure you, your sisters will do very well out of this. And," he continued, his voice dropping low, "if you end the engagement, then there will be scandal, shame and your sisters' chances of a happy match will fall significantly. I do hope you are aware of that."

Louisa opened her mouth to say something more, to try and find a way to beg her father to change his mind, but she could say nothing more for the Earl walked away from her directly, leaving the door to close behind him.

She was alone.

The Duke of Yarmouth? He is to be my husband? Louisa covered her face with both hands, tears beginning to fall again as she considered her future. The Duke of Yarmouth was, to her mind, the most selfish, arrogant, inconsiderate scoundrel she had ever had the chance to meet – and now he was the one she was to consider as her betrothed? She could not understand why it was that the Duchess of Yarmouth thought that she would be a good match for him, why she had gone directly to Louisa's father and spoken of such a thing, for they had only had one minor conversation and nothing more! Was the lady truly desperate to have her son wed?

"Yes," Louisa sniffed, dropping her hands and going to sit back down on the couch, her embroidery forgotten beside her. "Yes, that is precisely what she is." The Duchess of Yarmouth, just as every other mother would be, needed to see her son wed and the heir produced, so that the family line could continue on without concern and the title handed down. Could it be that the Duchess was as selfish as her son? She shook her head to herself at this thought, for the lady had not given that impression when they had first met but yet, all the same, she had thought to force this match upon Louisa?

And forced it must be, for if I end the engagement, then what hopes are there for Rachel and Ruth?

"Louisa?"

She blinked, trying to clear her vision as she looked at her two sisters. "Rachel? Ruth? I did not hear you come in."

"The gentlemen callers?" Ruth frowned, tilting her head as she gazed back at Louisa. "Is something wrong, Louisa? Do you not recall that we are to take afternoon calls?"

Louisa sniffed and shook her head. "No, I did not recall it."

"You have been crying." Rachel frowned, pulled out her handkerchief and handed it to Louisa. "You should wipe your face, if not go to splash water on it also. We do not want anyone coming to see us to think that you are upset!"

A heaviness sank into Louisa's spirits as she heard her sister's words, realizing that yet again, Rachel was thinking only of herself. Ruth said something that Louisa did not quite make out, though it sounded as though she was berating Rachel a little.

"I think I shall do just as you have suggested, Rachel." Getting to her feet, Louisa made her way to the door, her shoulders rounded and her steps heavy. "Forgive me for my melancholy state. I will come back as quickly as I can so that we do not miss any gentlemen callers." She did not listen to Ruth's words of encouragement to remain, to tell them why she was melancholy but instead, made her way out into the hallway. For whatever reason, she did not want to tell her sisters about their father's news, did not want to tell them a single word of what had been said. For the moment, it was her secret, a terrible and distressing secret that she hid in the very depths of her heart, knowing that one day soon, it would be told not only to her sisters but to all of society... and there would be no escaping it then.

Chapter Seven

Joseph scowled as his mother sailed into the room, a broad smile on her face. "Mother, please. I do not know why you are smiling when we are already tardy! Do hurry, the carriage is waiting by the door." He made to usher her out, only for his mother to stop him by simply lifting her hand, palm out, towards him.

"You are to be formally introduced to your betrothed this evening," she informed him, taking all of Joseph's irritation away in one swift moment and instead, replacing it with utter shock. "Whether or not you wish to make the actual announcement this evening, I shall leave it up to you, though I have already begun to make preparations for a ball. I do hope that with the engagement and the ball, the *ton* will begin to reconsider your character even if it still does leave a great deal to be desired."

Joseph swayed lightly, no longer feeling as confident nor as determined as he had been only a few minutes beforehand.

"Joseph?" His mother used his Christian name, her eyebrows lifting as Joseph blinked back at her, no words coming to his lips. "You are aware that I went to speak with the Earl of Jedburgh, are you not?"

A slow hiss of breath escaped Joseph as he tried to regain himself a little, only to see his mother's slow smile begin to spread across her face. Evidently, she was a little pleased that he seemed so off-balance, so surprised by her determinations. Perhaps this silence was not the reaction she had expected and, thus, she was a little relieved because of it.

"What did you do, Mother?" Joseph finally managed to say as his mother shrugged lightly. "I do not understand."

"Why do you not?" she asked, a slight hint of laughter in her voice. "You know what I was to do, do you not?"

"You went to speak with the Earl of Jedburgh but I did not think…. That is to say, I did not think for even a moment that you would be successful."

"And why not?"

Joseph's mouth opened and then closed again, the answer coming to him though he was unwilling to say it. The reason he had believed she might be unsuccessful – though there had been a great concern that she might be able to wrangle her way into some sort of agreement – had been solely because of his own reputation and because of his behavior. Now, it seemed, that was no great concern to the Lord Jedburgh, who had agreed that one of his daughters *would* marry Joseph.

"I cannot be betrothed if I have not accepted it," Joseph tried to say, putting a strength into his voice that he did not truly feel. "And I tell you now, I do *not* accept it."

"Yes, but you shall." Just as Joseph had put a force into *his* voice, so now did his mother do the same. "That is precisely why we are here in London, is it not? And you have disgraced yourself a good deal already, I believe. Quite why you would wish to add to that disgrace, I do not know."

Joseph flung up his hands, trying to ignore the way that her words bit at him. "Mother, I have been forced to come to London by your own dreadful behavior and thereafter, now, you insist that I do yet more to quieten you!"

The Duchess took a step closer to him, one finger pressing lightly against his heart though her eyes were like shards of glass, breaking into his skin. "I do not care whether or not you think ill of me in this, I only care about you taking on the responsibility that you ought. You *are* going to accept this engagement and you *will* make the announcement this evening, else I shall. Do I make myself quite clear?" She glared at him for another long moment before turning on her heel and marching out of the room, leaving Joseph to stare after her, still overcome with shock at what was now being laid out for him.

After a moment, he closed his eyes tightly and groaned, rubbing one hand over them as he fought to come to a clear understanding of his future. He had two choices. Either he could do as his mother asked, could accept the engagement and make the announcement, or he could refuse to do so and turn his back on it all. The first would bring him to a place of dissatisfaction and dislike, for he certainly did not want to be married and had no desire to take care of a wife, but the other would bring him the same agonies as he had endured over the last few months with his mother, if not a good deal worse! If his mother would return to her ways of making his life nothing but misery and trouble, then he would have to simply tolerate it for as long as he could or take his leave of the estate for as long as he could – which would be difficult given his business affairs and tenants... Though he had not given much thought to the latter of late, Joseph acknowledged.

"I do not think I can bear it," he muttered, pushing his fingers through his hair, only to let out a groan as he realized he would have made a mess of his carefully brushed hair. Making his way across the room to where a large mirror hung on the wall, he took in his reflection before making a few adjustments, making certain that he appeared to be just as well as any other, save for the paleness of his features and the fear lurking in his eyes.

Joseph scowled hard but the image remained. He was not the tall, confident gentleman he had always known. Instead, his pallor was dull, his eyes holding shadows and lines pulling across his forehead. His shoulders were a little rounded, as if he were hunching in order to protect himself in some way from the burden now placed upon them. Closing his eyes, Joseph tried to keep the fight going, tried to let his heart rage over what his mother had done but found, instead, that there was a dull weakness there. It was as if he did not want to fight anymore, as though he was giving up and accepting his fate. It was not a pleasant feeling and it was certainly *not* what Joseph wanted to do but the more he considered it, the more he realized that it would have to be so.

He would have to accept. He would have to marry... but he did not have to be the sort of husband that the lady might be expecting.

A hint of a smile touched the edge of Joseph's lips, though it held no mirth within it. *I shall make it quite clear to this young lady that I have no interest in matrimony, that I do not intend to be any sort of husband to her.* The smile continued to grow, his shoulders pulling back just a little. *I will be just as I have always been. A wife does not mean that such things must cease, does it?* With a nod to himself, Joseph turned on his heel and strode away. *And, if I am lucky, she will be the one to end the engagement rather than I and all will be well.*

***

"I am to meet her this evening." Joseph said to his friend after entering the ballroom.

Lord Quillon's eyebrows lifted. "And you have no notion as to who she might be?"

Joseph shook his head. "No, none. All I know is that her father is the Earl of Jedburgh – and yes, I know that you are vaguely acquainted but no, I do not know which daughter it is to be."

"I presume, the eldest?"

A cold hand grasped Joseph's heart and he shook his head. "I do not know. Did you say that none of them are wed?"

His friend nodded. "From what I recall, none of them have made a match as yet this Season, though the youngest is only just out."

Joseph's eyebrows lifted. "The youngest out? The elder two unmarried?"

"Yes." Lord Quillon spoke slowly, dragging the word out as he thought. "Yes, that is so, I am sure of it." His expression cleared. "The younger only just made her debut. I know because I was there."

Chuckling, Joseph threw his friend a questioning look.

"Yes, yes, I will admit to being there solely to take note of the young debutantes who had come to join society for the first Season," Lord Quillon laughed but not before he had gone a little red. "It is important to know who is present, that is all, especially if one is interested in taking a bride!"

"Oh, yes." Joseph's smile faded. "I had forgotten that you were intending to do such a thing as that this Season."

This time, it was his friend's turn to chuckle. "Ah, but you have quite forgotten that it will be you first of all who shall wed, my friend! Yes, I shall wed also but not before you!"

This made Joseph's whole body tremble though he did try to hide it from his friend. He did not want to marry, did not want to take a bride and yet, it was a decision he was making to follow through with what his mother had arranged. "I am quite sure I shall not be the sort of husband that *you* shall be, however," he said, quite plainly. "You will be honourable, kind, considerate and caring. I intend to make my betrothed fully aware that I will be none of those things." He laughed as he said this but Lord Quillon did not so much as smile. Instead, a frown began to spread across his forehead, a line forming between his brows as he looked back at Joseph, a heaviness coming upon his features which, in turn, seemed to sink into Joseph's soul.

"I confess, I am surprised to hear that you intend to be so dark and deceitful a fellow," Lord Quillon replied, as a knot tied itself in Joseph's stomach, realizing that he had lowered himself in his friend's opinion. "The way you speak is not the way my friend spoke when I first left for my Great Adventure. Yes, you were a rascal but I did not think you heartless."

"I..." Joseph opened his mouth and then closed his again before letting out a long sigh, shaking his head. "You know that I do not want to marry. I hope that, by informing my bride of this, she will be the one to step away from me and thus, end the engagement."

"And that way, you will be free of it and then, might I ask, if you believe that your mother will simply give up?"

With a shrug, Joseph nodded. "I would hope so."

"Then I think you are a fool, both in how you are approaching this and in your belief as regards your mother's great strength of mind and her clear determination," came the reply. "I understand that you do not wish to wed, my friend, but you *are* accepting this betrothal regardless. I do not think that you are then able to continue to blame your mother for it, since you yourself have accepted it. And, thereafter, might I suggest that there are benefits to being a married gentleman, benefits that you might not otherwise have considered?"

Joseph snorted, rolling his eyes. "I hardly think that any benefit of matrimony will outweigh the enjoyment and the pleasure I have at the present moment."

This time, Lord Quillon let out a bark of hard laughter, making Joseph feel rather small, aware that his own remarks had been a little derisory.

"Ah yes, I forgot about your present *enjoyment* of society

and how well they think of you," Lord Quillon replied, his jaw tightening just a little, his eyes flashing. "How there are more in society who wish to avoid you than to draw close to you. Are those the enjoyments of which you speak?"

It was the first time in their friendship that Joseph felt them close to an argument and even to a parting of ways and, having no desire for that, he took in a deep breath and then let it out slowly. "Quillon, I –"

"There you are." Before he could continue to speak, his mother interrupted them both, casting an apologetic glance towards Lord Quillon. "Come now, your betrothed is waiting."

Joseph blinked quickly, seeing his friend turn away, clearly finished with their conversation. "My betrothed?"

"Your betrothed?" Someone from behind him exclaimed aloud, only for Joseph to turn and shoot them an angry glance, making the young lady eavesdropping let out a squeak of embarrassment. It did not stop her from immediately then whispering to the lady beside her and Joseph quickly made his way through the crowd, fairly certain that the *ton* would now know of his engagement before he even had a chance to meet his betrothed. His heart hammered wildly, his stomach twisting this way and that as he continued towards the side of the ballroom, where it was a little quieter. His mother cast him a glance over her shoulder, a smile on her face but questions in her eyes – perhaps afraid that he would say or do something that would end the engagement before it had even begun – but Joseph gave her only the smallest nod.

"Here we are." His mother stopped, smiled and then moved to one side, letting Joseph step closer to the small circle of people. "Lord Jedburgh, might I present my son, the Duke of Yarmouth? Yarmouth, this is the Earl of Jedburgh."

Joseph took in the gentleman opposite him, seeing him a little diminutive in stature, his eyes heavy and showing no sort of deference as he held Joseph's gaze. "What a pleasure to meet you, Lord Jedburgh," Joseph said, bowing, as the fellow only inclined his head rather than bow.

"I have heard of your reputation, Your Grace, but I have been assured that you will be considered when it comes to my daughter," the Earl said, his words bold and holding a great deal of weight which fell upon Joseph without warning. "I would not like her to have the *ton*'s mockery surrounding her because of you."

"I quite understand." Joseph did not say anything more, refusing to permit himself to agree to anything he had no intention of doing, allowing his gaze to shift to the first young lady beside the gentleman. "Might I ask if –"

"I am the one you are betrothed to, Your Grace."

Joseph turned his head, only for his breath to catch, his heart coming to a stop for just a moment as he took in a familiar face. Blue eyes held his, brown curls dancing lightly about her shoulders as she lifted her chin. Her face was pale, no color in it whatsoever but there was a steadiness to her that spoke of determination.

Joseph did not know what to say.

"You are astonished, I see," Lord Jedburgh murmured, though Joseph could not tear his gaze away from the young lady. "I do hope that you find my daughter's beauty acceptable, Your Grace. Your mother appears to be quite convinced that she will make you an excellent match."

This made the young lady's lip curl for a moment, though she quickly pulled that from her expression and instead, looked away. Joseph's heart plummeted to the ground, then ricocheted back up, making him feel a little nauseous. It could not be! Out of all the young ladies of London, he had never once imagined that this creature, this forceful, outspoken, fiery young lady would be the one he was meant to marry!

"We... we have met before," he managed to say, his voice rasping. "I did not know that... that is to say, I was unaware of her title."

"Louisa!" One of the other young ladies elbowed her and immediately, Louisa's face went bright red, only for the Duchess to speak quickly and firmly, casting Joseph a look as she did so.

"What my son means is that there was an incident in which he injured your sister, that is all," she said, directing her gaze now towards the other young lady. "He apologizsd – eventually – and thus, that is why he does not know her title. Though now, of course, I am glad to be able to present to you Lady Louisa, daughter of the Earl of Jedburgh."

Joseph knew what was expected of him, understood that he was meant to reach out his hand to the young lady and bow over it but instead, found himself so breathless with shock that he could only stand there, staring at her. Lady Louisa, however, dipped into a proper curtsy, then held his gaze, one eyebrow lifting as she waited for him to respond.

"I do not think that we can wed," he said, a little hoarsely. "I do not think that –"

"I believe that we are already engaged, Your Grace, whether you might wish it or not," came the response, as Lady Louisa interrupted him. "Now, are you to take me a turn about the room so we might acknowledge it to all of the *ton* for, given the amount of looks we are garnering, I believe that the news is already out."

Joseph swallowed hard, his mind telling him to run, to escape from it all and to turn his back entirely on the engagement and on Lady Louisa. Instead, however, he found himself offering her his arm and, without another word to her, began to lead his betrothed through the crowd of guests.

His life, as he knew it, was now over.

Chapter Eight

Louisa glanced up at the Duke of Yarmouth, her mouth dry as she fought to think on what it was she might say to him. When her sisters had been informed of her news, they had been just as stunned as Louisa had been, meaning that neither of them had found anything whatsoever to say for some time. Once the gentlemen-callers had quit the room that afternoon, Louisa had broken down into a flood of tears and that in itself had been enough to bring her sisters rushing over to her, doing their best to comfort and support her. It had been a very sweet moment, despite the sorrow that her heart was filled with, for she had seen her sisters in a new light. They had been kind, caring and gentle and had clearly seen her pain and sorrow. They had asked her if there was a way for her to break this engagement, to refuse to do as their father had arranged but even in asking that question, Louisa had seen in their eyes that they already knew the answer. Thus, she had dried her tears and silently determined that she was going to do whatever she could to make the best of things – and that meant accepting that she was to wed the Duke of Yarmouth.

"You are as astonished as I, I presume." The Duke shot her a glance and then lifted his head again, his chin a little higher than before. "I do not want this betrothal and I certainly do not want this marriage."

"And you think that I am eager for it?" Louisa could not keep the sarcasm from her voice. "In all of my years of hoping, I have only ever longed to be wed to a gentleman who is considered a rogue by all of society and who, I know, will care nothing for me."

The Duke's jaw tightened. "I do not think you need to speak in as caustic a manner as that."

"Nor do you need to speak in as brash a manner as that," Louisa returned, sharply. "Do you think that I need to know that you do not want this engagement or this marriage? It is as apparent to me by your manner than anything else." A sudden tightness came into her throat just as tears began to burn in her eyes. "I am about to have all of society's sympathy and yet, there is nothing I can do about it."

With a scowl, the Duke blew out a breath of obvious frustration. "It is a most ridiculous situation. Neither of us wish to wed and yet we both must do so."

"It is what it is." Louisa pushed back her tears and forced herself to lift her chin. "I have been told what is expected of me and therefore, that is what I shall do."

"I am afraid I am not as willing as that."

Something curled in Louisa's stomach. "You mean to say that you will end this betrothal before it has even begun?" She did not know whether she was happy or upset over that, relieved that she would be free from him but also concerned as to what the *ton* would think of the betrothal ending so quickly. Would she be spurned? Would they think poorly of her for it? Or would it be that they would understand and she would not be rejected? Thinking on this, Louisa frowned. She did not want anything to affect her sisters' chances of making an excellent match.

"I have no intention of ending our engagement." The Duke stopped walking suddenly, making Louisa stumble, though her hand on his arm prevented her from falling. Turning almost entirely towards her, he looked back at her with a steady gaze and with two lifted eyebrows. "*You* shall do it."

Louisa could not speak for some moments, staring back at the Duke with nothing but utter astonishment coursing through her. The Duke's eyebrows lifted all the higher as though he were waiting for her to respond, to say yes or no to this decision of his and Louisa, tugging her hand from his arm, immediately shook her head.

"I certainly shall not!" she exclaimed, a vision of her sisters and all the mockery that would come to them should she do such a thing rushing through her mind. "I have absolutely no intention whatsoever of breaking apart our betrothal, no matter how much I might wish for it to be so!"

"But why not?" the Duke asked, coming a little closer to her as the other guests swirled between them. "You seem to have a fairly reasonable grasp of my character and therefore, you know the sort of husband I shall be. Why, then, would you not do such a thing?"

Louisa swallowed tightly, glaring back at him. "Because," she began, keeping her words as strong as she dared in company, "I have other people that I consider. I have a responsibly to my sisters and I will *not* endanger their chances of a good match simply because of my selfishness!" Her lips pinched. "It may be that you do not understand such a thing, given that you appear to have no scruples whatsoever and certainly do not think of anyone else."

She watched as the glimmer of hope left the Duke's expression, only for him to scowl darkly at her. He opened his mouth but then closed it again, his jaw flexing as if he had wanted to give a retort but could not.

"Shall we dance?"

Louisa blinked in surprise, only for the Duke to grasp her hand and tug her towards the dance floor. Much to her surprise, she was set back from him as he then bowed, ready to step forward and take her into his arms. A thrill of pins and needles raced up her arms and into her neck, though it was not a pleasant feeling.

"I am not particularly enamoured with dancing," she murmured, as the dance began, leaving Louisa and the Duke as part of a small group of dancers as they each took turns in the set. "Would that you had asked a little more politely."

The Duke chuckled but it was not a warm sound. "I hardly think that you need to be told that I am not a gentleman who considers such things," he said, taking his steps with her before turning to the other lady beside him. That lady, Louisa noticed, looked up at the Duke and then let her gaze drift to Louisa when the Duke set her back, having clearly overheard the whispers from the other guests at the ballroom of their engagement. Louisa was forced to remain silent as the Duke had some more steps away from her, though she did not look up at him nor smile when the turn came for her to dance with him again. She did not like this, almost hated every moment that she was forced to be near him. He had shown her no kindness nor had even attempted to understand her present feelings on their engagement. Instead, all he had done was talk about himself and practically demand that *she* be the one to end their betrothal so that he did not have to.

"Tell me," she murmured, as the Duke returned for her,

clasping both of her hands in both of his, "why do you want *me* to end our engagement? Why can you do not do such a thing?"

The Duke stepped away from her. "I have my reasons."

"But none that you will share with me? I who is to be marrying you?"

With a nod and another shrug, the Duke stepped away to dance with the lady while Louisa was turned by the other gentleman, but she barely managed the steps. It was as if the air around her was turning stale, as though the light from the candles was soon to be extinguished given the dimness of the room. She was breathing quickly now – a little too quickly – as what felt like ice began to run through her veins. Her mind filled with visions of what it would be like to be wed to the Duke – no pleasant thoughts – and as the Duke reached for her hand again, it took all of Louisa's inner strength not to yank it back again.

"You understand, I am sure." The Duke smiled but his eyes narrowed. "I am a Duke and I have had enough said about me by the *ton* already. I cannot permit them to say more for then..."

He trailed off but anger flashed through Louisa's mind as she recognized what it was he was saying. "But then if the *ton* say more of you, you will have even less opportunity to return to your roguish ways, will you not?" she said, hoarsely, as the Duke's eyes caught hers again, his lip curving at the edge. "You will have even fewer young ladies willing to be pulled into your arms."

"I *am* glad that you understand me so well," the Duke murmured, as he stepped back to bow, the dance – much to her relief – now coming to an end. "I do hope that you will, therefore, do as I ask?"

Louisa did not even curtsy, such was her shock. The Duke of Yarmouth was the very worst sort of gentleman, it seemed, for not only was he making it clear that yes, he was a scoundrel and yes, he was thinking only of himself, but also wanted her to accept that and, indeed, to do what she could to support him in his venture! It made her stomach twist, her whole body flooded with a sense of heat and then a rush of cold as she closed her eyes tightly.

"I cannot." Her heart cried out but she brought her sisters to mind, reminding herself of their standing and how important it would be for *them* that she continue on with the betrothal. "As much as I might wish to, I cannot."

The Duke's expression darkened immediately. Perhaps he was used to everyone doing as he asked at once – especially young ladies – but Louisa was not about to give in to him. "Then, Lady Louisa," he said, his voice low and filled with anger, "I shall do everything in my power to force you to do so."

At this, he turned on his heel and strode to the other side of the ballroom, leaving Louisa to stand alone in the center of the room. All of the other ladies were being led away by the gentlemen that *they* had danced with, but she, it seemed, was to be left to find her father or sisters alone. Shame burned in her cheeks as she tried to keep her head held high, demanding silently that a light smile lift her cheeks so that the *ton* would not think she was upset. Out of the crowd, a gentleman came forward to her, stopping directly in front of her, though Louisa did not know who he was.

"Lady Louisa, I presume." He inclined his head. "Do permit me to take you *back* to the dance floor for the next dance?"

Louisa blinked rapidly, keeping back her tears. "Forgive me," she whispered, her voice trembling as she tried to fight the swell of emotions. "I do not think we are acquainted and – "

"Let us pretend that we are so that the Duke of Yarmouth's behaviour does not shame you in the way that I believe he intended." The gentleman smiled gently though there was a spark of anger in his eyes. "He and I are friends, you understand, so I am aware of his present... disinclination to his new state."

"Friends?" Louisa asked, hoarsely, the corners of her vision blurred just a little as she held back her tears.

"We were." The gentleman scowled. "I am not certain that I would call us as such, given his behaviour. However," he continued, calming his expression, "I should like to come to your aid. The *ton* will be watching. If they think that you were waiting for me to come to take you to the floor, then they will not think that the Duke has neglected you utterly and you shall bear no shame."

Swallowing hard, Louisa dropped into a quick curtsy, closing her eyes just as two tears fell to her cheeks. She dashed them away quickly, hoping that no-one but the gentleman before her would have noticed them. "You are very kind, sir."

"The Marquess of Quillon," he told her, offering her his arm. "Now come, let us hope that I recall the steps of this dance! The last thing I wish to do is embarrass you, I can assure you! Thereafter, I will help you find your family again. All will be well, I promise you."

Taking in a deep breath, Louisa tried to assure herself with those words but all the same, the fear of what the *ton* would think of the Duke's and her connection given what they would have witnessed continued to wind through her. It was not until she began to focus on the steps of the dance that the fear slowly began to leave her and, by the end of the dance, she was feeling a good deal better.

Though, she considered, as she curtsied to the Marquess of Quillon, that did not give her any aid when it came to the Duke of Yarmouth. How could she bring herself to marry such a cruel, selfish gentleman? And just how much more would he make her endure in his hope that *she* would be the one to end their betrothal?

Chapter Nine

"Whatever is the matter with you?"

Joseph jumped violently as the door to his study flew open and the Marquess of Quillon stormed into the room. "I – I beg your pardon, Quillon? Whatever do you mean by storming in here and –"

"Leaving Lady Louisa to stand alone on the floor as you did last evening? Do you have any sort of notion as to what that did to her?"

Joseph pushed himself out of his chair, a little unsteadily given the surprise in how his friend had rushed into the room. "Quillon, I hardly think that *you* need to concern yourself with either the lady or with my own behaviour. It is nothing to do with you and –"

"Indeed, it is necessary that someone convey to you the most lamentable nature of your comportment, and if I do not undertake this task, then who shall?"

A scowl wrapped around Joseph's expression. "My mother is one person enough, I assure you. I do not require *you* to also –"

"What you think you require and what I know you require are very different." It was the third time that Joseph had been interrupted and he felt his scowl darken while, inwardly, feeling a light twist of discomfort over his friend's words. Last evening, he knew he had behaved disgracefully towards Lady Louisa and had felt a twinge of guilt in leaving her as he had done but what else had there been for him to do? He needed her to end their engagement. Behaving in such a way was the only thing he could think to do, given that she had otherwise refused.

"Are you even listening to me?" Lord Quillon threw up his hands. "When I returned from my Great Adventure, I was told about your exploits but never did I think that you would surpass the rumours that had been spoken about you!"

Pain flashed through Joseph's heart but he ignored it. "I do not think you have any right to speak to me in such a way," he grated, angrily. "We may well be friends but that does not mean you can pass judgement over my behaviour!"

"Did you not *see* the look on Lady Louisa's face when you stepped away from her?" his friend demanded, seemingly ignoring everything that Joseph had been saying. "Did you think about what it might be that she would feel? Or are you so utterly selfish and inconsiderate that the only person you think about in all of this is yourself?"

Joseph could not give him an immediate answer. Instead, he looked away, his jaw tight and his hands curling into fists as he tried to ignore the guilt which stabbed through him.

"She was crying, Yarmouth."

Another shock rushed over Joseph as his gaze shot towards Lord Quillon, whose expression still held nothing but fury. His hands were at his waist, his jaw set, his eyes flashing – and yet another stab of guilt went through Joseph's heart.

He steadfastly ignored it.

"This young lady clearly does not want to marry you, either," Lord Quillon continued, when Joseph did not answer. "I saw her as you and she danced together. There was no joy there, no hope nor expectation. Instead, there was only despair."

"She made it very clear to me that she did not want to marry either," Joseph answered, attempting to fill his voice with confidence though it did not do as he had wanted. "I suggested that she end the engagement but she would not."

"Why was that?"

Joseph lifted his chin and shrugged. "Something about her sisters, I believe."

Lord Quillon threw him a scathing look. "And you did not listen carefully enough to hear precisely what it was, I presume? Too engrossed in contemplating your own situation and how you might extricate yourself from it. You expect her to do as you wish, expect her to follow through with whatever circumstance will suit *you* best and when she does not, you try to shame her into action." He snorted, shaking his head, his hands falling to his sides. "I have no desire to be associated with you any longer, Yarmouth. I am utterly ashamed to have once called you my friend."

Shock stole all of Joseph's words as he stared back at Lord Quillon, his eyes rounding. He tried to speak but no sound came out, tension beginning to flood through his frame.

"You will tell me, no doubt, that we have been friends for a long time and, had you been of a different character, then we might well be so now. However, when I saw the look on Lady Louisa's face last evening when I told her we were friends, I knew then that something had to change." He shook his head. "I am in search of a bride, of a love match, if you must know and I will not have my reputation damaged because of my association to you."

"Quillon!" Joseph tried to laugh, shaking his head. "Pray, tell me, can it be that you are in earnest regarding this matter? It is not as though I am some dreadful sort who has sullied many a young lady now, is it?"

His friend's eyes narrowed. "How am I to know how many young ladies you have taken into your arms?"

Joseph swallowed tightly, trying to find a way to explain to his friend that he had never deliberately determined to pursue any young lady that was a debutante, though, given the look in Lord Quillon's eyes, he did not think that it would be of much use.

"I am not as poor a character as you think," he said, trying to sound determined but realizing that his words were falling short. "I know that I have done many a thing that *you* might not have done but that does not mean that our friendship is worth nothing, surely?"

Lord Quillon lifted his chin. "Had you been the same fellow you were when I first left for my Great Adventure then yes, we might well still have been friends. But I cannot and will not maintain a friendship with a gentleman who treats those around him with contempt, who thinks only of himself and cares nothing for those that he injures. I have never deliberately set out to shame a young lady in order to have her do as I ask. I have never seen a young lady cry because of my behaviour and I certainly will not maintain a friendship with someone who can be both so callous and so careless with it." He inclined his head, his expression one of disgust. "Good afternoon."

"Quillon, I –"

His friend had quit the room before Joseph could say anything more. The door closed and Joseph was left staring at it, his mind struggling to come to terms with what it was that he had just been told. He did not want to accept all that Lord Quillon had said to him about himself, did not want to take in those words and yet, they lingered there in his mind, regardless. Closing his eyes, Joseph dropped his head and rubbed one hand over his eyes.

Am I truly so terrible?

A memory of Lady Louisa's expression as he had informed her about what it was that he required of her came back into his mind with such force, Joseph sucked in a breath. He had demanded that *she* be the one to break the engagement and when she had refused, he had been angry with her. Angry that she would not do as he had asked and irritated at her refusal to accept his reasons for the responsibility to be hers alone.

"I have every right to be angry," he said aloud, though his words seemed to burn on his lips, forcing him to reconsider. Ever since he had stepped out into society he had found that almost every young lady of his acquaintance had done as he had wished them to do. That was when he had begun to realize just how much he had available to him, just how much he was able to take for himself without too much consideration about the ladies themselves.

And that is the reason that she irritated me so much, Joseph considered, scowling. *Because she would not do as I asked of her.*

The door opened before he had even time to align his thoughts, his mother coming into the room with her eyes flashing. Joseph's defenses rose as she stood, her elbows akimbo, her face white save for a dot of color in each cheek.

"Lord Quillon has informed me that he will not be returning to this house," she said, crisply. "And he has informed me about why that is. I know you will, no doubt, want to blame him for speaking of you in such a way but have every assurance, I pressed him until he did so. I would not let him leave until he explained all – and I cannot quite believe what it is I have been told."

Darkness cast a shadow over Joseph's soul. "I have disappointed you yet again, it seems."

"Disappointed?" The Duchess shook her head. "It is more than that, my son. I think I am at an end."

Joseph frowned as his mother dropped her hands to her sides, a sudden weariness about her. "What do you mean?"

"I mean that I am at an end of all of this," she answered, shaking her head as a long sigh escaped after her words. "I have done all that I can to try and set you back on the right path, to make you into the sort of gentleman that your father wanted you to be, the sort of gentleman that I could be proud of. But I see now that it is quite without hope. I will gain nothing from this endeavour save for disappointment and sadness. Therefore, Yarmouth, I am at an end." She flung out her hands, her lips thinning for a moment as she held his gaze. "Do as you please. Whether you wish to keep the betrothal or end it, I cannot bring myself to care any longer. You have brought enough shame to Lady Louisa already – in only one single evening – that she will have every reason to end your connection anyway and if she does not, then that is to her credit and certainly *not* to yours." With another shake of her head, the Duchess turned back towards the door. "I think I shall go to reside with Lady Newhampton."

"Lady Newhampton?" Joseph repeated, astonishment flooding his voice. "Why should you go to reside at the house of your friend when you have a perfectly adequate house here?"

His mother glanced back at him, though she did not stop walking away from him. "The company there is a good deal better, Yarmouth."

"But... but the *ton*!" Joseph exclaimed, something like dread grasping at his heart. "They will hear of this! They will know that you have quit this house so you might then stay with another and, no doubt, they will then speak of it. That, I know, is not something that you want."

The Duchess shrugged. "I do not think I have too much concern in that regard any longer," she said, reaching the door and stepping out of it, her words drifting back towards him. "I have endured enough already. What more can another whisper do?"

It was as though the entire room had filled with a cold, winter wind as Joseph watched his mother walk away from him. He did not know what to do, did not know what to say. Instead, his heart pounding as though he had been in some great exertion, he sank back down into his chair and closed his eyes.

I am alone.

The thought was not a pleasant one and Joseph shuddered

lightly, opening his eyes and trying to take in a long, steady breath. The truth was, he told himself, he had merely caught the displeasure of the *ton* and that would soon fade, no doubt when they found someone else to be upset with. As for Lord Quillon, if he did not want to maintain their friendship because of some sort of misplaced concern over his own reputation, then that was his own concern. His mother, Joseph told himself, had always been overly concerned with Joseph's present state and his character and she was, therefore, overreacting entirely.

"There is nothing for me to be concerned about," he told himself, ignoring the twist of worry and the stab of conscience which came at the very same time as he rose out of his chair. "I shall take myself into town and prove that it is not as bad as they say"

With a nod to himself, Joseph made his way to the door and, pausing only for his hat and gloves to be brought to him, chose to hail a hackney rather than wait for his carriage. Yes, he thought, a walk about town would prove to him that all was quite well and it was both Lord Quillon and his mother who were overacting.

He had nothing at all to worry about.

***

That is the third cut direct I have received thus far.

Joseph's spirits were slowly sinking as he attempted to smile at two young ladies who were walking together. One, however, simply turned her head away while the other caught his gaze. Her eyes rounded though it did not seem to be in either pleasure or delight given the way she did not smile and, instead, pulled her gaze away from him as quickly as she could. What was worse was that they both then moved to the other side of the street, as though to stay as far from him as possible.

"Whatever is the matter with them all?" Joseph muttered, trying to set aside the desire to climb into a hackney and return home all at once. This was not at all what he had expected. Yes, he knew that society as a whole did not look favorably upon him but there had always been some who would speak with him, who would smile and laugh at what he had to say, who would welcome him into their company. Now, however, Joseph began to fear that there would be very few who would do such a thing. Was he to be considered an outcast, then? Would the regular invitations he received to various occasions begin to slow until he received none whatsoever? The thought was a dreadful one and Joseph's jaw tightened, a slight tremble in his frame that he did not particularly like. He had always been strong, had always been determined to do whatever it was he wanted and without concern, but now, to be stuck in this moment, he felt as though he were quite lost. This was not what he was used to when it came to society, not what he wanted from them. Could it be that Lord Quillon had been right in all that he had said? Was the Duchess also correct to state that he was not pleasant company? Joseph did not know what to think, rubbing one hand over his eyes as he continued to meander through the busy streets of London.

"Did you hear what he did to Lady Louisa?"

Joseph spun around, only to catch the eye of a young lady who was then whispering to another, though she merely met his gaze and then continued speaking as though he was not standing right there, hearing her every word.

"He left her standing on the floor after their dance, going to find someone else to speak with instead!"

"Goodness!" The other young lady looked at Joseph with darkness in her gaze as they walked straight past him. "How dreadful."

"It is just as well Lord Quillon came to her aid," he heard the first young lady continue, now as they walked ahead of him. "He is an excellent gentleman, I must say."

"And the Duke of Yarmouth is quite the opposite!"

Those words struck Joseph so hard, he felt as though he had been punched hard in the gut, pushing him backwards. Warmth washed over him, only to be followed by an icy coldness. Every part of his body shook, his eyes blinking furiously, panic seeming to swirl around him.

I am nothing like Lord Quillon. He closed his eyes, swallowing repeatedly, his hands clasping and unclasping as he fought to regain his composure. *And now no-one in all of London wants anything to do with me.*

Chapter Ten

The relief which washed over Louisa when she saw Lady Julia was so great, she felt tears spring into her eyes. "Julia. How glad I am to know you are here."

"And you are more than welcome to stay with me for this evening's soiree, should you need to," Lady Julia replied, quietly, taking Louisa's hand and squeezing it. "Are you quite well?"

Louisa nodded, trying not to let the memories of the ball rush into her mind and overwhelm her. "I have my two sisters here this evening also, of course. I must make sure to take care of them." Her lips twisted for a moment as she saw Lady Julia frown. "Father has not stepped into his responsibilities towards them despite the fact that I am now betrothed," she explained. "Though there is certainly more interest in our family now."

Lady Julia scowled. "Which will be good for them, I am sure, but not necessarily for you." She looked carefully into Louisa's face, as though trying to make certain that she truly was as well as she had said. "The ball was last week now, was it not? Have you seen him since then?"

Louisa shook her head. "And I have no desire to."

"I quite understand."

"I did see Lord Quillon again, however," Louisa continued, "and I thanked him for his kindness." Seeing how her friend's expression immediately softened, she tilted her head just a fraction. "You have been in his company again recently, also?"

A touch of color came into Lady Julia's cheeks. "We were not acquainted until he brought you to my company on the night of the ball but yes, since then, we have been in conversation a few times. I think him an excellent gentleman."

"I quite agree." A small tug of sadness on Louisa's heart made her smile sorrowfully. "Would that I could say that about my own betrothed."

Lady Julia's frown returned. "You are still going to marry him?"

Spreading out her hands, Louisa let them fall to her sides as she sighed. "I have no other choice. If I refuse, if I end the betrothal, then all that will bring will be disaster."

Her friend's frown lingered. "And by that, you mean your sisters."

"I do."

"You cannot always think of them, you know." Lady Julia tossed her head. "It seems to me as though you are never to be truly considered, my dear friend, as though you will never have anyone truly care for you!"

"I have you." Louisa tried to smile but it was something of a sad one, her gaze tugging away as Lady Julia's words burned into her soul. That was precisely how it felt, for though Ruth was kind, neither Rachel nor Ruth were truly able to sympathize. They were both now considering what might happen to them, given that Louisa was to marry the Duke of Yarmouth – and that had come about simply because Louisa's father had given *her* no consideration when it came to matching her with a rogue! The Duke himself did not care one iota for her or for her feelings, that much was apparent and thus, the only person Louisa could think of who truly cared for her was her dear friend.

But even Lady Julia could not stop the match.

"I think that – "

"Lady Louisa, there you are. I have been looking for you these last few days but have not managed to find you. Might I speak with you for a few minutes?"

Louisa bobbed a curtsy, her heart suddenly twisting. "Your Grace, good evening. Might I present my friend, Lady Julia? Lady Julia, this is the Duchess of Yarmouth."

"The Duke of Yarmouth is my son," the lady clarified, as she curtsied towards Lady Julia. "A son who has brought me nothing but mortification and upset, just as he has done to you, Lady Louisa." She turned back to Louisa, her eyes holding hers. "I come to you to apologise."

"Apologise?" Louisa repeated, a little surprised. "I did not think that you had done anything wrong, Your Grace! At least, certainly not to me."

"Ah, but I have." The Duchess set a hand to Louisa's arm, her eyes still holding fast to Louisa's. "I was the one who approached your father, who asked that you become engaged to my son. Had I not done anything of the sort, then you might now be a good deal happier rather than carrying such a heavy burden of embarrassment and sorrow." She took in a deep breath and released Louisa's arm. "I thought that you would be an excellent match for my son because I have never seen anyone speak to him in the way that you did. However, I did not account for my son's selfishness and arrogance and, in that, I believe that you have been grievously injured. If there was something that I could do to free you from his arm in such a way that would not bring your family any sort of damage to your reputations, then I would do so."

Louisa, recalling that she had once wondered whether or not the Duchess of Yarmouth was as selfish as her son, felt shame bite hard at her. "Please, Your Grace, you need not feel any sort of guilt in that regard."

"Oh yes, I do." The Duchess frowned slightly. "I am fully aware of my own inconsideration. I did not think that your father would be as willing as he was to consider you as a match for my son so quickly but it appears that I was wrong in that regard. As I have been wrong in all of this, unfortunately."

Louisa's heart squeezed with a sudden sympathy for the lady. She could scarcely conceive of the burden the Duchess must bear, enduring such shame on account of her son's unseemly behaviour. That had to be something of a trial, at the very least.

"There is nothing that I can do save for trying to convince my son to end the betrothal," the Duchess continued, her eyes a little glassy now, clear emotion written there. "I know that he has expected *you* to be the one to do it and I greatly admire your refusal. I know that it comes from a consideration of your other responsibilities."

"How... how do you know all of this?"

The Duchess smiled, albeit a little sadly. "I am a Duchess, Lady Louisa. It does not take much for me to be able to find out whatever I wish from whomever I wish. In this situation, however, it was Lord Quillon who told me all. I understand that he is just as upset as I am over the Duke's behaviour towards you and he has, in addition, ended his friendship with him."

Surprise caught Louisa's breath for a moment. "He has?"

"Oh yes." The Duchess smiled again but it did not reach up into her eyes. "Perhaps my son will now begin to realise just how poorly he is thought of here in society and it might, though I doubt it shall, bring him to truly consider his selfishness and his arrogance. I must hope that, with myself stepping back from him also, he will end the betrothal and set you free."

"Stepping back?" Louisa blushed as the Duchess' eyebrow lifted. "Forgive me, I do not mean to pry."

"No, not at all." The Duchess laughed but it was a sad sound. "I thought I had explained myself clearly but it seems I have not." She took in a deep breath. "I am to stay elsewhere for the remainder of the Season. Thereafter, I think that I shall remove to the Dower house, even though my son is not yet married, simply because I believe that I would enjoy my own company a good deal more than the company of my son. I shall no longer pressure him to marry, shall no longer even encourage him to do so. He is free from all of that. Therefore, there can be no reason for him not to end the betrothal."

"I see." Louisa let out a slow breath, a sense of relief curling around her heart. "Then our betrothal may not stand much longer. There will be some rumours and whispers that follow, no doubt, but if the Duke is the one to end our connection, then –"

"I have no intention of ending our betrothal."

Louisa let out a gasp of surprise, whirling around to see the Duke of Yarmouth standing a little behind her, his arms folded across his chest and his brows low. Quite how long he had been standing there for, she could not say but the thought that he had been listening to their conversation was not a pleasant one.

"Are you eavesdropping?" The Duchess came to stand closer to Louisa, almost in a protective manner. "Lady Louisa and I were speaking privately."

"About me. You were speaking about me."

"As is almost half of society, so it should not come as any surprise to you." The Duchess arched an eyebrow as Louisa swallowed hard, still unsteady from the surprise of seeing him. "You say you will not end the betrothal? Why? You can have no reason not to!"

The Duke's chin lifted just a little, his gaze settling on his mother and then turning to Louisa instead. "We are just now engaged. The *ton* know of it and there is to be a ball thrown in our honour, is there not? I can hardly decide to end our connection before the ball and to do so thereafter would cause a great many people in society to whisper about me, would they not? And to whisper about Lady Louisa and her family and, given that her sisters are still to be wed, it would not be fair nor right for them to be affected in such a way. Thus, the engagement will stand."

The faint hope which had begun to pull into Louisa's heart immediately sank low as she took in the Duke's firm gaze, dark expression and obvious determination. She did not understand why he had decided to continue on with their betrothal when he so clearly had the opportunity to free himself from her. This explanation made very little sense, coming from a gentleman who had never given any real thought to the *ton* nor to his reputation beforehand. Why should he do so now?

"You do not care about my sisters," she found herself saying, the bluntness of her manner seeming to surprise the Duke given the way his eyes rounded. "You did not even listen to me when I first expressed my reasons for refusing to end our betrothal – in fact, you dismissed all that I said and practically berated me for considering them and my own standing! And yet now, you appear to be standing here and informing me that my two sisters – sisters that you do not know the names of, no doubt – are a consideration when it comes to our engagement?" She shook her head. "Forgive me, but I do not think that I believe your words to be true."

The Duke grimaced. "And yet, I find that I care very little as to whether you believe me or not, Lady Louisa. This is what I have decided and this is what shall be."

"Can you do it, then?" When the Duke frowned at her question, Louisa tried to explain herself again. "Can you tell me the names of my sisters?"

The frown the Duke wore dug all the more deeply into his forehead. "Their names are irrelevant to me. You are right to say that the ending of our betrothal would affect them."

Louisa did not know what to say, her mouth falling open in shock, though she shut it quickly. This was not the Duke of Yarmouth, not as she knew him! Why was he pretending now to be so considered, so caring over her two sisters and, in doing so, refusing to end his engagement to her? It was so simple for him to do, for if *he* ended it, then the *ton* would think poorly of him rather than of her and given how much stain his reputation already wore, what difficulty would that be for him to bear a little more?

"You are much too confusing, Yarmouth." For the first time in some minutes, the Duchess spoke up, though her voice was soft now, filled with the very same confusion that Louisa herself felt. "I give you the chance to break your engagement, I tell you that I will no longer berate you for your lack of responsibility in this matter and instead of accepting that and joyfully breaking the connection between Lady Louisa and yourself, you determine to continue on with it? To marry?"

"Yes, I do. And I shall." The Duke sniffed, then looked to Louisa. "Might we take a turn about the room, Lady Louisa? And perhaps, we should also stand up to dance."

Everything in Louisa pulled back from him as she shook her head. "I shall not dance with you, Your Grace. Not after what you did to me the last time we stood up."

The Duke inclined his head. "I give you my word, I shall not do the same thing again. I shall be the most perfect gentleman that has ever graced the floor."

Louisa shook her head again. "I do not believe you."

"Please." The Duke took a step closer to her, his eyes searching her face and, for what was the very first time since the beginning of their conversation, Louisa saw something else there in his eyes. It was not the arrogance she had expected, nor the boldness which he carried about himself. Instead, there seemed to be some sort of desperation in the way that he looked at her, in the way the edge of his voice curled up as he spoke.

"Please, Lady Louisa. Let me prove to you that I shall not do such a thing again," he said, moving closer to her again. "I see that what I did in stepping away and leaving you alone was very wrong indeed. It must have been mortifying for you."

"Which was precisely what you wanted."

The Duke shut his eyes tightly, his jaw flexing for just a moment. "Yes." The word came out heavy, as though he had to force himself to say it. Opening his eyes, he took a third step closer to her and Louisa shivered lightly, a little unwilling still to be near him. "I will not do such a thing again."

He is asking me to trust him. The realization made her want to laugh aloud for what sort of gentleman would do such a thing after behaving as he had done? Was she truly to believe that, this time, he would not treat as he had done before, simply because he said he would not? "Is this not yet another ploy to try and embarrass me, Your Grace?" she asked, as the Duke shook his head. "Is this not another way for you to bring me so much shame, I will do whatever I must to end our betrothal?"

"I need not do such a thing any longer." The Duke gestured to his mother and, frowning, Louisa glanced to her. "My mother will not push me into matrimony any longer, that much she has said. There is no reason for us to remain connected and yet, I have decided *not* to end our betrothal."

"Perhaps you do not want the *ton* to continue to think poorly of you. In ending the engagement, they would add another stain."

The Duke's lip curled. "Stain upon stain."

Louisa tilted her head just a little, looking at him. This was all most peculiar, all very strange indeed and yet there was something about the way he spoke and the desperation that she saw in his expression that made her want to believe him, albeit with a good deal of caution.

"I confess that I do not understand him, so I cannot give you any advice." The Duchess's eyes sharpened as she looked at her son. "Though all the same, I would be careful."

"Mother, please." Casting an angry look towards her, the Duke shook his head. "I know that you have every reason to be frustrated with me but I am being truthful here. I understand that you may not be able to accept that nor believe it but, for the first time in a long time, I am being entirely truthful."

Louisa swallowed tightly, looking from the Duchess to the Duke and back again. "I – I will walk with you, Your Grace," she said, after a few moments of consideration. "The dancing, however, will have to wait. I cannot bring myself to step out with you again and I pray that you will not force me to do so."

Both of the Duke's eyebrows leapt up at once. "I should

never force you, Lady Louisa."

"Nor coerce me?"

At this, the Duke's head dropped instantly, his gaze falling to the floor. Louisa was surprised to see him appear so shamefaced but quickly reminded herself that the Duke was a gentleman who would try to garner whatever he could from whomever he wanted in whatever way he chose! That did not mean that this show of regret was in any way genuine but might very well, in fact, be nothing more than a show.

"I will not coerce you." Taking in a deep breath, the Duke lifted his head. "I will *not* coerce you, I swear it. I give you my word."

"Which means nothing to her, I hope you understand?"

The Duke closed his eyes again as the Duchess' words hit him. Louisa said nothing, however, watching as the Duke's expression grew pained, clearly a little upset with what his mother had said to him. Or was it just an act?

"I am aware it means nothing at present," he said, eventually, his voice rasping with what sounded like a heavy weight of emotion. "But I have nothing else to offer."

Louisa considered, taking in all that he had said and though she felt herself reluctant, chose instead, to step forward and take the Duke's arm. "I will not change my mind about the dancing *this* evening," she explained, looking up into his face. "I may not change my mind about it in the days or weeks to come! I am afraid, Your Grace, that I have no trust in you whatsoever. I do not say this to pain you but it is the truth and I will never shy away from that. I cannot tell whether you are serious in what you say or if you intend to do something all the more dreadful to me in order to force my hand."

The color pulled itself from the Duke's face as he looked at her, giving her a nod and pulling his eyes from hers. Louisa, all the more astonished at his pallor, said nothing but, with a nod of thanks to the Duchess – who was watching her son with slightly narrowed eyes – permitted him to lead her away and back out onto the floor. Whether he would prove himself to do and to be all that he had said, Louisa did not know, but in her mind, she highly doubted it would be so.

Chapter Eleven

Joseph walked with Lady Louisa on his arm but felt not even the smallest hint of joy. The way she had spoken to him, the doubt in her eyes and the distrust in her expression had confirmed to him what he had already learned the previous day: he was of despicable character. He had spent the previous night and day lost in confusion, trying to hold onto his arrogance and pride and yet being forced to face the truth – that no-one in society wished to be in his company and that his character was so loathsome, he had lost not only the company of a dear friend but also his mother! If one's mother turned their back, then that was serious indeed!

"Lady Louisa, good evening."

A young lady stepped close to Lady Louisa but threw only a scathing look towards Joseph, reaching to take Lady Louisa's hand. "Do you need me to walk with you?"

Lady Louisa smiled but did not refuse the offer as Joseph had hoped. Clearly, this young lady did not want to be in Joseph's company but he himself was eager to walk alone with Lady Louisa, even if only for a short while. It was as though the world had been turned upside down in a single day, for now, not only did he yearn for her company, but also felt compelled to demonstrate that he would not resort to the very tactics he had once employed to shame her into acquiescing to his demands. It was as though, in seeing how the *ton* viewed him, he had been shamed into seeing just how dreadful a person he truly was. Trying to claw back some sort of vague semblance of a good reputation seemed futile but it was all he could think of to do.

"Lady Julia, permit me to introduce you to the Duke of Yarmouth."

Joseph quickly bowed though the young lady did not curtsy.

"We have already been introduced, though it was some time ago and it is clear you do not remember me, though I should not be surprised about that, given your reputation."

Joseph bristled instantly, still entirely unused to having young ladies such as her speaking to him in such a manner, though

Lady Louisa was still just as blunt and forward as she had always been.

"No, you should not," she agreed, as Joseph quickly threw aside his upset, reminding himself that he had no reason to be angry at the truth being spoken to him, even if he did not like it. "However, given that he is my betrothed, please do try to be pleasant, Julia."

Lady Julia snorted. "I do not think that you should marry him, Louisa. He is not a good character and – "

"I do not think that sort of discussion is needed here," Lady Louisa broke in, surprising Joseph at her determination. "Please." She smiled, only for her gaze to go to the left of Joseph's shoulder, her smile growing. "Ah, Lord Quillon. Good evening."

A twinge of nervousness rose in Joseph's heart as he turned around to see his former friend approaching, though the gentleman did not look at him at all. Instead, he turned his attention solely to Lady Julia and to Lady Louisa, never once glancing at Joseph himself.

"Good evening." Lord Quillon bowed but still, did not look at Joseph. "How glad I am to see you both here again this evening. I must hope that your dance cards are not yet *entirely* filled for I should very much like to dance with you both!"

"I should be delighted!" Lady Julia was the first to offer Lord Quillon her dance card, though Lady Louisa bit her lip, clearly a little uncertain as to what she ought to do.

Joseph scowled. "If you wish to dance with Lord Quillon, despite the fact that you have already refused me, then I shall not prevent you, Lady Louisa. I shall not make a single word of protest, for, as I have said, I am very well aware as to why you do not have such a desire."

The smile that spread across Lady Louisa's face was a delightful one, though Joseph noted, it was not directed towards him. What felt like disappointment crashed over him and he closed his eyes, dropping his head as Lady Louisa handed her card to Lord Quillon. Something in him wanted her to have that same enthusiasm for *his* company, wanted to see her eyes light up as she gave him her card but instead, he was left with only disappointment and shame.

"I am not in the least bit surprised that you did not want to dance with the Duke, though I am grateful for your consideration of me." Lord Quillon sniffed and then glanced to Joseph for what was the first time since he had joined the conversation. "Good evening, Your Grace. Thank you for permitting your betrothed to dance with me."

"I do not give her my permission," Joseph snapped, upset at how Lord Quillon had spoken to him. "She does not require it. Lady Louisa is well able to do just as she pleases."

Lord Quillon blinked, then lifted one eyebrow. "Is that so?"

"His Grace is trying to convince me that he has altered his character somewhat, you see." Lady Louisa replied, with the boldness that he had come to expect from her. "This has only been revealed to me this evening and thus, I am more than a little uncertain when it comes to a request to stand up with him again."

Joseph closed his eyes, wishing that Lady Louisa had not spoken of such a thing to anyone. "Which I have assured you I quite understand," he said, a little harshly still. "Lord Quillon, I will repeat that I do not require Lady Louisa to ask my permission to dance with anyone. She may do as she chooses."

Lord Quillon's head tilted just a little. "An altered character, you say?" he murmured, clearly having only considered Lady Louisa's words rather than what Joseph had said. "And what has brought that about, might I ask?"

Closing his eyes and aware that there would be plenty of others around him who would be hearing parts of this conversation, Joseph's jaw tightened. "It is not something I wish to discuss here at present."

"Indeed."

Seeing the slight curl of Lord Quillon's lip and the doubt in the single word Lord Quillon had spoken, Joseph lifted his chin. "But I can assure you, I mean every word. I am sure that neither of you – the three of you, in fact – have no reason to believe anything that I say. However, be that as it may, I am determined to prove myself to all of you."

Lord Quillon looked away, turning his attention to Lady Julia. "A very swift change of heart, it seems."

With a harsh clearing of his throat, Joseph practically

demanded that Lord Quillon's attention returned to him. "Yes, I will admit that it has been. Though that might be expected, when one loses not only one's closest friend but also the love of their own mother. In addition, when one realises that the *ton* as a whole has turned against him and that the only young lady who might give him even a modicum of her attention is the one now forced into a betrothal with you, then yes, that might well bring about a change of heart… or a new realisation as to just how dreadful a character one has."

This speech not only brought about a turning over of Joseph's heart as he spoke words of truth and hard realizations but also made Lord Quillon, Lady Julia and Lady Louisa stare at him with wide eyes, none of them speaking for some moments. Joseph, flushing hot, ran one hand over his hair and then turned away, choosing to step away from Lady Louisa entirely. He had no expectation that Lord Quillon would believe him, expecting instead that his friend would not be able to trust his words, just as Lady Louisa had done. Lady Julia's opinion he did not know but he was fairly certain that it would be similar to the other two. An uncomfortable prickling ran down his back as he walked away, certain that three sets of eyes were fixed to him but Joseph did not turn his head.

Suddenly, the only place he wanted to be was at home, away from the scrutiny of others, away from the dark looks which chased after him, from the dislike he felt pouring out of Lady Louisa and even Lord Quillon. Shame was not a feeling that he often endured but at this moment, it appeared to be practically pouring over him, soaking him through. Dropping his head, Joseph hurried to the door, out into the dark night and without even summoning his carriage, began to walk in the direction of home.

Chapter Twelve

Louisa frowned as she accepted the bouquet of flowers from the footman's hands. "Was there a card or a note with them?"

The footman nodded. "Yes, my lady." Plucking it from his pocket, he handed it to her before turning to take his leave, having been dismissed by a nod from Louisa. Setting the card down, Louisa turned the bouquet around in her hands, taking in the different kinds of flowers, the scents and the colors and, despite her uncertainty over who had sent them, she did begin to smile. It was a very kind gift and she certainly did value it.

"Here." Gesturing to the maid who had come to join her in the drawing room should any gentlemen come to call, Louisa handed the flowers to her. "Please put these in water and then send for my sisters. They should be ready by now and can come to sit with me for the afternoon callers. "Louisa was sure there would be a good many visitors but whether or not any of them would be acceptable as potential suitors for either Ruth or Rachel, she could not say. Some, Louisa was certain, would come solely to see her, to try and garner some information about her betrothal to the Duke of Yarmouth which could then be fed to the others in society as rumor. Those were the last sort of gentlemen she wished to be in company with her sisters!

With a sigh, Louisa picked up the card and opened it, her eyes rounding in surprise as she read the few short words there.

'*I have not done as I ought. I beg your forgiveness.*"

It was signed by the Duke of Yarmouth but whether or not it was truly from his heart, she could not say. Yes, there was a part of her that wanted to believe him but there was another part – a larger part – that told her he was nothing but a liar and a deceiver. She could not give him her trust instantly, just because he had assured her of his change in character now, could she?

And I hope he does not expect that either.

"What beautiful flowers!"

The door opened and both Rachel and Ruth hurried in, with Ruth's eyes going straight to the vase of flowers that the maid had now set on the table. "Who are they from?"

"My betrothed." The word seemed to stick to her tongue but she spoke it anyway. "The Duke of Yarmouth."

Ruth's nose wrinkled, though Rachel only nodded and then went to sit down on one of the couches, obviously disinterested.

"I do not know yet if I can trust him," Louisa said, firmly. "Now you must not question me on that but you *must* question the motivation of any and all gentlemen who come to call on you, especially if they are those who begin to ask you questions about the gentleman that *I* am courting. It may well be that they are seeking out only gossip rather than truly caring for you."

Ruth nodded solemnly but Rachel only rolled her eyes. "Louisa, I am sure that the gentlemen who come to call are all excellent fellows. We are well able to attract that sort of gentleman on our own, rather than being forced to marry a gentleman we know nothing about."

Her cold words sent a shudder up Louisa's back but she kept her mouth shut, refusing to let her sister's words bring out any anger in her. She had enough to manage already.

"Rachel, you need not be so callous! I think that –"

A knock at the door had Louisa silencing her sisters quickly, gesturing for them to be quiet and to stand at a seat. She too hurried to join them before calling for the door to be opened, fully expecting someone to come in who had come to call on either of her sisters.

"The Duke of Yarmouth, my lady." The butler came in, opened the door wide and Louisa's heart clattered to the floor, practically feeling her sisters' disappointment.

"Your... your Grace." Louisa swallowed tightly, bobbing a quick curtsy. "I – I did not think – "

"It is the first time I have come to call on you, yes. I am well aware that you would not have expected me to do such a thing." The Duke's voice was low, heavy with something that Louisa could not quite make out. Disappointment, perhaps? Sadness? Or was it that he was irritated at being forced to come to call on her, given that it would be what she and society might expect?

"Please, do sit down." Louisa gestured to the seat near her, then nodded to the butler who quit the room in order to bring the tea trays in. "Thank you for the flowers. They are quite beautiful."

The Duke nodded but said nothing and a silence fell across the room. Louisa twisted her fingers in her lap, not certain what to say and feeling a deep sense of uncertainty over what she ought to do next. She had no conversation to make, no tea to pour as yet and it seemed that the Duke himself had nothing that *he* wished to speak of either! Why had he come to call? Was this one of the ways that he desired to prove himself to her? Prove that his character had changed? Pressing her lips together, Louisa looked back at him, their gazes meeting. Louisa did not pull hers away, however, taking him in. His expression certainly seemed a little darker than before, his brows heavy over his green eyes – green eyes which now seemed closer to brown than to green given the weight they held. Black hair fell carelessly over his forehead, his strong jaw tight as he let out a slow breath – and something in Louisa trembled lightly. He *was* a handsome gentleman, she could not help but admit that but as to his character, she could not give him even a little of her trust as yet.

"Lord Quillon and Lady Julia appear to be very... happily acquainted." Finally, the Duke spoke and Louisa could only nod, having no desire to speak of her friend to the Duke. Yes, Lord Quillon did appear to be very happy in Lady Julia's company and she the same, but that did not mean that Louisa felt able to comment on it.

Another knock came and Louisa let out a breath of relief, glad that the tea was about to be brought in so she would have something to do. However, though the butler did step in, it was only to announce the arrival of both the Earl of Huntly and the Viscount Proudfoot – both gentlemen that Louisa had been introduced to some time ago. Louisa got to her feet quickly, as did her sisters though Louisa caught how Rachel's eyes lit up, her smile growing as she looked to Lord Proudfoot.

"Good afternoon." Louisa glanced to her sisters, seeing them curtsying. "Please, do come to join us. Might I ask if you are acquainted with the Duke of Yarmouth?"

Both the gentlemen glanced at each other, then nodded, though a flicker of interest came into Lord Huntly's eyes... something that Louisa did not particularly appreciate. She did not want to have to spend her afternoon trying to quell any sort of whispers and rumors that the gentlemen might carry with them out into London society.

"How very good to see you, Lord Proudfoot," Rachel exclaimed, her cheeks a little pink as she resumed her seat. "And to you also, Lord Huntly."

"Indeed, it is very kind of you to come to call on us." Ruth, her voice soft and, to Louisa's sharp eyes, a hint of concern in her expression, also sat back down. "It has been some time since we have spoken, however, is it not?"

Lord Huntly put one hand to his heart. "Much to my chagrin, of course," he said quickly, though Louisa quickly understood the reason for her sister's concern. If Lord Huntly had not shown any interest in either Rachel or Ruth in some days, then what was the reason for his arrival now? Could it be that he wanted only to talk about the Duke of Yarmouth? "I do not mean to interrupt your conversation, however. I will only stay if the Duke of Yarmouth is contented to have us stay."

The Duke sniffed. "It makes no difference to me."

Seeing the maids coming in with the tea trays, Louisa gestured to them quickly, feeling a knot tie itself in her stomach as the tension became a little more palpable – at least, to her. Yes, the Duke did not seem to mind in the least at having more company but she certainly did although Rachel seemed quite delighted at Lord Proudfoot's presence. Mayhap he had come to call with good intentions but Louisa was not at all sure about Lord Huntly.

"I must say, I have heard a good deal about you of late." Lord Huntly gestured to the Duke as he spoke, making the knot in Louisa's stomach tighten though she looked both to Ruth and then to Rachel to see which of them would pour the tea – but both did not catch her gaze, given that their eyes were fixed to either Lord Huntly or Lord Proudfoot. Sighing inwardly, Louisa set to the task, praying silently that the Duke would not continue on the conversation but would set it to something else.

"I am sure that you have." The Duke's voice was low though his gaze was sharp, his eyes narrowed just a little as he looked back at Lord Huntly. "However, I –"

"I have to tell you that this latest rumour is certainly quite extraordinary! I do not think that I have heard anything like it before!"

Louisa's hands shook suddenly and the teapot almost slipped from her fingers. A light sweat broke out across her forehead as she continued to pour the tea, wondering what on earth it could be that Lord Huntly had heard.

"I hardly think that this is the time nor the place to discuss such things," Lord Proudfoot interjected, his brows knotted as he took the teacup from Louisa with a nod of thanks. "Lady Rachel, might I ask if –"

"What nonsense!" Lord Huntly laughed aloud, slapping his knee as though Lord Proudfoot had said the most ridiculous thing. "I am sure that the ladies have all heard of this already! That is why you are here, is it not, Your Grace? You have come to reassure Lady Louisa, your betrothed, that what is being said is entirely without substance, yes?"

Louisa continued to serve the tea, though as she handed the cup to the Duke of Yarmouth, he touched her fingers with his for just a brief moment, making her head lift and her eyes look straight back into his. Her stomach twisted sharply, her breath catching as she lingered, trying to understand what it was in his gaze.

"I have not done anything worthy of rumour," he said, speaking to Lord Huntly but keeping his eyes fixed to hers. "I can assure you, whatever has been said, it has no truth to it."

Blinking, Louisa turned to serve the tea to her sisters, understanding now that the Duke of Yarmouth wanted to tell her, albeit indirectly, that there was no truth in whatever was about to be said – but Louisa's heart dropped low. He was asking her to trust him, was he not? And yet, she could not simply do that because he asked her to. There was nothing like that between them, not as yet. Whatever Lord Huntly was about to say – for he would say it regardless, she was sure – Louisa was more inclined to believe it rather than to trust the Duke.

"Are you quite certain?" Lord Huntly chuckled and Louisa closed her eyes, her face growing hotter and hotter as a sudden silence fell. It was quite clear to her that Lord Huntly had come for one reason and one reason only and that was so that he might be the one to inform both her sisters and herself about what he had heard about the Duke. No doubt, he now wanted to see what their reaction would be so that *he* could then go and spread that news around London. How much better it would be for him now that the Duke himself was present!

"I do not think that you ought to speak of such things, Lord Huntly." It was Lord Proudfoot's quiet voice that broke the quiet, his steadiness something that Louisa appreciated, though she could not bring herself to lift her head and look at him. All she could do was look down at her tea cup, waiting for the blow to fall. "It is quite clear to me that no-one present wishes to hear it."

Lord Huntly laughed harshly. "It is quite apparent to me as to why the *Duke* would want to keep such a thing secret! Though I think it unfair that you should tell your betrothed, Your Grace, since it will mean a significant lack for her once she becomes your bride."

"A lack?" It was Ruth who spoke up, only for her face to turn scarlet as Louisa looked back at her sharply, wishing that she had kept her mouth closed.

"Yes, a lack!" Lord Huntly laughed again and Louisa's hands curled into fists, keeping herself silent with an effort. She wanted to rise to her feet and demand that Lord Huntly take his leave at once but, in doing so, she would, no doubt, present yet more fodder for the *ton* to take a hold of. Lord Huntly would not be shy in sharing that with anyone!

"Huntly, I –"

Lord Proudfoot's words were interrupted by Lord Huntly's loud, firm voice, telling them all just what it was that he had heard.

"The Duke of Yarmouth has been heavily involved in gambling of late, given that the *ton* have been so disinclined towards his company! It seems that he has been seen frequenting gambling dens all across London and, it is said, has lost a great deal of his fortune!"

Louisa stiffened but kept her expression as blank as she could, refusing to look at Lord Huntly as he spoke.

"It seems that liquor and cards do not go well together, Your Grace," Lord Huntly finished, with another laugh. "Just how much have you lost?"

"Nothing."

The answer brought a sudden rush of quietness as Louisa finally found herself able to lift her gaze and look back at the Duke as he spoke. His eyes were fixed to Lord Huntly, his face black with anger and Louisa, though she herself was not the cause of his upset, found herself shuddering.

"That is nothing but a lie," he continued, his lips thinning. "I have been doing nothing of the sort."

"Is that so?" Lord Huntly sat back in his chair and tilted his head to the left, seeming almost amused at the Duke's reaction. "I am not surprised that you have refuted it, of course. Though that does not mean that I believe you." One hand gestured towards Louisa. "Neither does it mean that your betrothed does either."

Louisa lifted her chin. "I would ask you kindly not to speak about me in such an informed manner when you are entirely *uninformed.*"

This seemed to dim the smile of Lord Huntly just a little, his eyes darting between Louisa and the Duke. "Then do you mean to say that you trust the word of the Duke of Yarmouth?" he asked, a faint hint of mirth still in his voice. "Come now, Lady Louisa, the entirety of the *ton* knows that you have been forced into this betrothal by the demands of your father and that you have no true feelings for the Duke of Yarmouth – and none could blame you for that, given the way that he left you alone on the dance floor and went in search of *other* company, if you garner my meaning." A broad smile flicked across his face for a moment before fading away. "You need not pretend, not with me."

Not knowing what it was that drove her, Louisa found herself on her feet, her gaze fixed to Lord Huntly, her hands down by her sides though still held in tight fists. "I think that such questions are both rude and improper, Lord Huntly and, has been told to you by Lord Proudfoot and the Duke himself, there is no requirement nor desire to hear such rumours – for that is what they are. They are nothing but rumour and I will not have any such things spoken here."

Lord Huntly blinked rapidly, his smile gone completely. "You mean to say that you trust the Duke's word over mine?" he asked, sounding utterly astonished. "I know that it is only a rumour, as you have said, but everything that has been spoken about of the Duke of Yarmouth thus far has been proven to be quite true!"

"And yet, that still does not mean that everything is," Louisa countered, knowing that she spoke against what was within her own heart. "Now, Lord Huntly, either you are here to take tea with us and enjoy good company or you are here to spread rumours and see what our reaction is to them. If it is the former, then you are welcome to sit here with us. However, if it is the latter, then I must ask you to take your leave at once." A thin smile pressed itself upon her lips. "I am sure that the *ton* will be very interested to hear of your purpose in calling upon us, Lord Huntly, should it be the latter. Do bear in mind that I have just as many people in society interested in what *I* have to say." She waited until Lord Huntly's smile had vanished completely, his face paling just a little before she sat back in her seat, turning to look to her sisters who were both seated with the same look of utter astonishment on both of their expressions. With a slight lift of her eyebrow, she caught both Rachel's eye and then Ruth's, encouraging them silently to begin a conversation and, much to her relief, Ruth soon did.

Louisa did not pay much attention to the conversation, however. She was much too busy thinking about what Lord Huntly had told her. Despite her attempt to convince Lord Huntly that she did not much care for what he had told her and that she trusted the Duke over his word, the truth was, she believed precisely the opposite. And if the Duke of Yarmouth *had* been frequenting the gambling dens of London, then just how much of his fortune was gone? Was it a vast amount? And what would that mean for her future?

"I think I shall take my leave." The Duke of Yarmouth rose to his feet, catching Louisa's attention and making her eyebrows lift in surprise as he bowed towards her. "Lady Louisa, might I ask if you would accompany me to the carriage? I know that you have a responsibility to your sisters but I am certain that both of these gentlemen will do nothing untoward in the few minutes that I will be gone."

Louisa swallowed tightly, glancing at her sisters who both nodded, though neither appeared pleased. "But of course. I shall send the maid in, however." Following after the Duke, she left the door to the drawing room wide open and quickly catching a maid's attention, sent her into the room thereafter.

"I thank you."

Glancing at the Duke sharply, Louisa tried to make out whether or not she could trust that the quiet, dullness of his voice was truly a representation of all that he was feeling or if it was just an act.

"I am sorry for what Lord Huntly said." The Duke looked at her as they made their way slowly up the hallway to the front of the house. "That is a rumour and nothing more, I assure you."

Louisa lifted her shoulders and then let them fall, saying nothing.

"I do not know why you said such things to Lord Huntly when I am quite certain they are untrue, but I am grateful to you for your consideration of me. It is not something I deserve, I know."

The Duke stopped walking and turned so that they stood face to face and something swept through Louisa with great force, stealing her breath for a moment as his eyes fastened to hers. She tried to speak but her words were gone from her, finding herself almost transfixed at the intensity of his gaze.

"I should like to prove to you that these rumors are untrue," the Duke continued, pulling his gaze away from hers and as he did so, finally permitting her to breathe. "If you would be willing to accompany me, I would take you to my solicitors and have them show you the recent accounts. That should be enough to prove that I have not done as it is being said."

"You know that I do not believe you, despite what I said to Lord Huntly?"

He nodded. "Of course. Why should you believe me? It is not as though there is any trust between us."

"I see." Louisa took in another breath, then shrugged again. "Your Grace, I said those things because I did not want Lord Huntly to go and spread yet more rumours through London – this time about me and my reaction to the news of your gambling. I was protecting myself, I suppose, as well as protecting my sisters."

For whatever reason, the Duke closed his eyes briefly as

though her answer had pained him in some way. "I quite understand."

"Though you do not need to prove anything to me," Louisa continued, quickly. "I do not think –"

"But *I* want to."

Without warning, the Duke moved a little closer, reaching to take her hand in his, squeezing it with a fervency she had not anticipated.

"I want to prove to you that I am not as the *ton* has been saying," he said, searching her face. "Please, if you would only accompany me, then I would be able to show you that it is not as they have said. That way, at the very least, you would be able to have full confidence when someone else speaks to you about it, as they will."

Louisa did not know what to say to this, hearing the urgency in his voice, the sound of gentle desperation in his voice and finding herself a little taken aback. This was not the Duke that she knew! The Duke of Yarmouth would not care about his reputation and would give no thought to what she herself considered when it came to his actions, so why now was he so desperate to have her believe him?

"I suppose that it would not be any sort of great trial to accompany you," she said slowly, as the Duke let out a slow breath of relief and then released her hand. "If you so wish."

"I thank you." The Duke of Yarmouth took her hand again but this time, only to bow over it. His lips were very close to the back of her hand and Louisa's breath hitched as warmth brushed across her skin, though he did not do anything other than bow. "Tomorrow?"

When he lifted his head and looked at her, Louisa suddenly could not breathe again. It was the second time that he had brought about such a strange sensation within her and though she nodded, she also quickly pulled her hand back to herself so that the sensation dissipated just as quickly.

"Tomorrow, then." With what was the first smile that had graced his lips ever since he had first come to call, the Duke inclined his head one more time and then stepped away, leaving Louisa with nothing but confusion, doubt and uncertainty lingering all about her.

Chapter Thirteen

"Here we are."

Joseph took the papers from his solicitor and scoured them before handing them to Lady Louisa. He watched her expression as she took them in, seeing the flickering in her eyes as she read all the numbers. He had every expectation that she was just as intelligent as he and could easily ascertain that all the transactions which had been written were correct.

"And this is all of them, up until the present day?" Lady Louisa asked, as the solicitor nodded. "Then you have not had any requests from the Duke of Yarmouth to take out some of his funds or to direct a significant amount to another?"

"No, my lady." The solicitor shook his head. "There is nothing other than what you can see here. The Duke of Yarmouth has always been diligent when it comes to examining his accounts and thus, we consistently strive to ensure that everything is transparent, up until the very day that he comes to visit."

Joseph managed to smile, a twist of nervousness in his stomach. "I do appreciate that," he murmured, "especially given that I came to call at an unexpected time."

The solicitor merely nodded though Joseph did catch the glimmer of happiness in the man's eye. He then turned his attention again to Lady Louisa, seeing how she continued to look through the papers before, finally, returning them to the solicitor.

"There are some rumours at present in London about me," Joseph explained, as the solicitor nodded, making Joseph a little suspicious that he already knew what Joseph was going to say. "They speak of an absence of sense when it comes to gambling and the like, stating that I have lost a good deal of my fortune. Given that I am soon to be wed, I wanted very much to reassure my betrothed that nothing of the sort has taken place."

The solicitor smiled briefly. "I do hope that you are reassured, Lady Louisa," he said, with a deferential bow of his head. "If there is anything else that I can assist you with, then please...?"

Joseph shook his head. "No, that is all. I thank you."

"Thank you." Lady Louisa, offering her own thanks, rose to her feet though she stepped out first rather than waiting for Joseph to do so. Joseph, after another nod to his solicitor, hurried out after her but she was already standing outside, waiting for him on the steps.

"Is... is something troubling you?" A little uncertain as to what might be wrong and what he ought to say given the tension and strain between them, Joseph did not make to climb into the carriage but instead stopped beside her, turning his whole body so that he could look into her eyes. Lady Louisa bit her lip, her gaze away from him and Joseph's stomach tightened. He did not know what it was that made her respond so, did not know why she appeared so ill at ease, especially after being reassured by the solicitor that all was well! Nor was he certain that it was his business to ask her such things, given that he was the cause of all her strife.

"Someone must have been spreading this rumor about you." Lady Louisa's clear blue eyes turned back to him, a faint hint of color dashing across her cheeks. "Someone has said something about you for their own reasons and that must be solely because of ill intent."

Joseph blinked, then frowned. "Or mayhap someone wishes simply to ruin my reputation further in the eyes of the *ton*. There can be no maleficence there, just a desire to add to the rumours already swirling, merely because the *ton* loves gossip and scandal! It does not mean that there is someone out in society eager to make certain that the *ton* thinks very little of me – especially given that they already do!"

Lady Louisa took in a deep breath and then let it out again, a faint line drawing between her eyebrows as she frowned. "That may be so, though I am not convinced by it."

"Does it matter?" Joseph found himself asking, as Lady Louisa's gaze returned to his. "I am already practically ruined in the eyes of the *ton* and everyone, most likely, feels nothing but great sympathy for you... as they should, of course." He shrugged. "If something more is going to be said, then what does it matter?"

"I – " Lady Louisa opened her mouth and then snapped it

closed before shaking her head, a flash of irritation sparking in her eyes. "I suppose that it does not."

Joseph hesitated, sensing that there was something breaking down between them, something that was drawing them a little closer together. It did not mean that they were friends nor did it mean that she was happy and contented with the situation but there was certainly less animosity, less uncertainty and for that, he was grateful.

"Should you like to get an ice at Gunter's?"

Her eyes flashed to his, widening just a little, her mouth forming a perfect circle for only a moment or two.

"You do have your maid and given that we are betrothed, it would not cause any sort of scandal." He did not know what caused the sudden urgency within him, the sudden rush of desire for her to accept, but it was there nonetheless. He pressed his lips tight together for fear that he would say more, not wanting to push her into accepting when she did not truly wish to.

"There could be no harm in it, I suppose." Lady Louisa did not sound in the least bit excited by the prospect and Joseph's eyes dropped to the ground, though he reminded himself that he had no complaint in feeling such a way. She had no reason to like him, no reason to want to be in his company, not after how he had treated her.

"You are aware that the *ton* will all be looking at us," he said, though he did turn to one side, in the hope that she would follow. "There will be many whispers and sharp looks."

Lady Louisa closed her eyes briefly, then set her shoulders back as though she was quite determined to do so, nonetheless. "Yes, I am aware of it. But since we are betrothed and since neither of us is going to end our engagement – not as yet, anyway – I suppose that I can accept that."

"Not as yet?" Joseph frowned as she fell into step beside him. "I do hope that you no not think that I have any intention of ending our betrothal, Lady Louisa."

"Why would I not believe that?"

Joseph cleared his throat gruffly, hearing the sharpness of her tone. "I can see why you would. However, I should like to make it abundantly clear that I have absolutely no intention of ending our engagement." A slight tremor ran through him as he realized the severity of what he had said, recognizing that now, he fully intended to stand up beside this young lady in church and offer her his vows. "I will not end our betrothal, Lady Louisa."

She looked up at him, a slightly quizzical expression on her face. "And is that solely so that you might garner the respect of the *ton*? Because you do not want them to think any worse of you? That is your only reason for continuing on with this arrangement?"

Joseph swallowed tightly but shook his head, finding it rather difficult to explain to her what it was that had driven him, especially when he himself was fully unaware. "It is true that I do not want the *ton* to think poorly of me, given that my reputation is already dreadful. However, as I am quite certain I have expressed previously, I possess no desire to continue being the sort of gentleman I have been until now." His shoulders lifted, the words coming slowly as he fought for them. "I suppose, what I mean to say, is that I do not want to be as cruel nor as inconsiderate as I have shown myself to be. For many years, I have thought of nothing and no-one apart from myself and it has only been with the loss of my dear friend's company and the awareness that my mother no longer wishes to be my company that has finally driven me to this change."

For some minutes, Lady Louisa said nothing. Once or twice she glanced up at him but still, she remained silent. Joseph too stayed quiet, not certain as to why she was so but feeling the heavy weight of her judgement settling upon him.

"This is not something that I can immediately believe, Your Grace, as I am sure you can understand."

"As I have said before, of course I do."

Lady Louisa nodded slowly, her curls dancing lightly in the breeze. Her eyes, whenever they caught his, were scrutinizing, as though she were thinking on not only all that had been said but on all that had taken place ever since the beginning of their acquaintance.

"The truth is," Joseph found himself saying, struggling to bear the silence and the searching gaze of her eyes, "I possess but a scant understanding of what it means to be a gentleman of admirable character. I have never truly embodied such a distinction, despite my father being an exemplary man of the highest regard. I confess to you that I have always thought of myself and the realization that I could do whatever I wished without too much upset from the *ton* because of my standing soon made me all the more inconsiderate! My mother has dealt with a good deal and in truth, I have never really thought about that until she told me she no longer wished to be in my company." Joseph shook his head, a sharp exclamation escaping from him. "Imagine, one's own mother no longer desirous of her child's company. That was a great shock to me, I must say, especially given that it came only a short while after Lord Quillon's remarks to me."

Lady Louisa nodded slowly. "You appear to be speaking the truth, Your Grace, and it is not the first time that I have heard you say such things. I am surprised that someone as assured as you would let his mother and his friend have such an influence upon him, however."

"But what else am I to take from it?" Stopping sharp, Joseph threw up his hands, turning on his heel so that he faced her. "I do not know what else I am to say! It felt as though all that I knew about myself, all that I thought I believed about society, was thrown upside down in one, heady moment – and it was not a pleasant feeling!" His hands fell down to his sides, his breathing quickening. "I saw myself as I have never done before: disliked, unwelcome and ill-considered. It was as though I looked at myself in a mirror and saw it shatter before my very eyes. Can you not understand how that has made me feel, Lady Louisa? Can you not see just how devastated that realisation has left me?"

Joseph, breathing hard, took a small step back from the lady, having only just realized that he had moved closer to her as he had been speaking. Lady Louisa's eyes were a little wider than before, her cheeks flushed but, as he watched, the surprise slowly left her expression and was replaced with only a brief hint of a smile.

"I think, for the first time, I may be inclined to believe you, Your Grace," she said, slowly. "It may take some time for any sort of trust to be built between us but either you are an exceptional actor *or* you are truly genuine in all that you have said."

Closing his eyes against the swell of emotion which rose in him – emotion Joseph did not understand precisely – he swallowed tightly and then let his hands go out either side before letting them fall again. "I am grateful for that at least."

"Then let us go and take our ice at Gunter's," Lady Louisa said, beginning to walk again. "Though mayhap, I might take your arm?"

Joseph's breath hitched, blinking rapidly for a few moments as he gazed down at her, barely comprehending. "My arm?"

"So we might walk together," she answered, her smile growing just a little. "I know that there is much to be built between us but this is a start, is it not?"

With a smile of relief etching itself across his face, Joseph moved closer and quickly offered her his arm which she took without hesitation. "Yes, it is a start," he agreed, a good deal more delighted with this small act than he had ever expected to be. "And a very good one at that."

Chapter Fourteen

Louisa stepped into the ballroom with her sisters on either side, her chin lifting as her heart clamored wildly within her, quite in contrast to the calm expression she set upon her face.

"Almost everyone near us is looking at you, Louisa."

"Yes, I am well aware of that, I thank you," Louisa murmured to Rachel, while Ruth rolled her eyes in her sister's direction. "Now, as I have already made clear, Lord Proudfoot is a gentleman well worthy of your company but Lord Huntly and any of his close friends are those that I would prefer you to avoid."

"And you would do well to listen to your sister in that regard."

A low voice from behind Louisa made her start, turning to see her father looking back at her.

"Are you quite able to chaperone your sisters this evening or would you prefer my company with you?"

All the more astonished at her father's consideration of her, Louisa paused before she answered, very well aware that her father desired only to be in the card room rather than at the ball itself but also, at the same time, thinking of her own circumstances. The *ton* would all be watching her, whispering about her and that would certainly cause its own difficulties.

"I would be glad to accompany Lady Louisa and her sisters around the ballroom this evening, Lord Jedburgh."

Louisa turned her head in the opposite direction, her heart leaping up – though she could not understand the reason for it – as her gaze fell upon the Duke.

"I saw you enter and came to greet you," he continued, looking at her as though he knew what she was thinking. "But if you would be glad of my company, then I would be happy to give it, though if you would prefer your father's, then – "

"Of course she would be happy to walk with you!"

Before Louisa could even speak, her father had interrupted, settling one hand on her shoulder. "I am grateful, Your Grace."

Louisa closed her eyes briefly, trying to push away the upset which roused itself over her father's lack of consideration. It was not even that he had spoken over her, more that he had spoken *for* her and had not once thought as to how she might be feeling.

"Forgive me if I seem impertinent, Lord Jedburgh, but I should like to hear what Lady Louisa herself has to say."

Another ripple of astonishment ran over Louisa's heart as she looked to see the Duke gesturing to her, though his gaze remained on her father.

"I have not been the very best of gentlemen and my conduct has given Lady Louisa every right to wish to stay away from me. I am fully aware of that and have determined to change but that does not mean that she has any reason to do as I ask. I do not mean to be impertinent but I should like to hear Lady Louisa's thoughts on the matter first."

Louisa's heart squeezed with a sudden sense of joy as she heard the Duke's words, appreciating his consideration of her more than she could express. Her father harrumphed but Louisa did not look at him, keeping her gaze firmly fixed on the Duke instead.

"You are most thoughtful, Your Grace, I thank you."

"Then are you contented, Louisa?"

Hearing the slight hint of irritation in her father's voice, Louisa glanced back at him. "Yes, father, I am contented to go with the Duke."

"Then I shall be in the card room," he answered, sniffing. "Good evening."

"Good evening," Louisa murmured, as her two sisters turned to look up at the Duke, both appearing to be a little astonished at just how much he had altered in his character. Louisa smiled up at him, herself surprised at the change in him but also in how grateful she was over his consideration of her. She could only hope it was genuine.

"I was just now reminding my sisters that Lord Huntly is not a gentleman that they ought to be in company with, though I have no concern over Lord Proudfoot." She tilted her head. "Unless you know something about the gentleman that I do not?"

The Duke smiled back at her, his eyes glinting. "I confess that I know Lord Huntly to be a gentleman of poor character, for he and I have often been in conversation – though it is clear that our connection means nothing given how easily he is willing to speak about me and the rumours surrounding me." He winced but then shrugged. "It is not something that I have any right to complain about however. I have no great character to stand upon."

"No, you do not." Ruth was the one to speak with tenacity, though she flushed as she spoke. "You must take care of our sister, Your Grace. Louisa has done a good deal for Rachel and for myself and not only that, she has given up more than she ought to have done. Our father, as you might well be aware, has no real interest in caring for his three daughters. Rather, he would prefer to give the responsibility to Louisa, when she should have been the very first of us to make a match here in London."

Louisa smiled at her sister, though she felt a flush of embarrassment climb up into her cheeks. Ruth, she knew, was the one who understood – more so than Rachel did! She saw what it was that Louisa had missed out on, understood what it was that Louisa had been forced to give up and now was clearly concerned that the Duke himself would not realize it. Louisa appreciated her consideration and her strength in speaking though she did not need Ruth to defend her so.

"Thank you for sharing that with me, Lady Ruth." The Duke spoke quietly and with a gravity in his voice that Louisa had not heard before. "I have tried to convince your sister that I have no desire to be as I had previously been any longer but I am also aware that it will take a good deal of time before that trust is built. It is the same with you and with you also, Lady Rachel, I understand but I will do my utmost to prove it."

Rachel only shrugged and looked away, though Ruth smiled a little carefully, her gaze flicking to Louisa for a moment.

"I do think that – " Louisa began, reaching to take the Duke's arm, only for another voice to interrupt them both.

"Goodness, are you still engaged to this rascal?"

Heat flared in Louisa's chest as she twisted around to see an older lady sending a sharp gaze towards her, her thin lips tight.

"Lady Brackensill, good evening." The Duke, clearly recognizing the lady, bowed quickly, then gestured to Louisa. "Might I present Lady Louisa and her sisters, Lady Ruth and Lady Rachel."

Louisa dropped into a quick curtsy, noting out of the corner of her eye that Rachel had fallen out of their little group and was now in conversation with another gentleman and two young ladies, though she did not make to move away. "Lady Brackensill, how very good to meet you," Louisa murmured, her heart beating a good deal more quickly as she lifted her head. "Yes, as you see, I am still betrothed to the Duke of Yarmouth."

"Then I must consider you foolish!"

Louisa frowned, aware of the mortification she felt at being spoken to in such a way but, at the same time, a sense of indignation rising within her. "Your opinion is your own, Lady Brackensill." She wanted to say more, wanted to demand that the lady fall silent but recognizing that it would be best to be as polite as possible, forced a small smile.

"I can understand your opinion also, given my reputation," the Duke added, sounding a little heavy-hearted. "However, I –"

"Not only your reputation but your continued dark deeds," Lady Brackensill interrupted, her shrill voice making Louisa wince inwardly, silently praying that it would not attract too much attention, though that seemed unlikely. "I have heard of them all! I have heard of your gambling and your lack of fortune, which is the most disgraceful thing any gentleman can do with the fortune that has been given to him."

Louisa lifted her gaze to the lady. "That is false, Lady Brackensill. I apologise for speaking so forcefully, but I have seen with my own eyes that such rumours are entirely unmerited. There is nothing in them but the tangled mess of whispers that society has breathed into them. The Duke has not lost a great deal of money, he has not gambled foolishly and he certainly has not lost the security of his funds for the future. I have seen his accounts, gone through them with his solicitor and can promise you that there is nothing of truth in what has been said."

This made Lady Brackensill take a breath, her eyes landing on the Duke's face before returning to Louisa. "Is that so? He has shown you his accounts, has he?"

"Yes. He has." Louisa moved to stand a little closer to the Duke, surprised to note that she felt a sense of protection over what was being said of him which was utterly ridiculous given the sort of gentleman he was! "The Duke's fortune is as strong as it ever was. I have no concerns in that regard."

Lady Brackensill moved a little closer to her, her voice now low and thready, her eyes narrowing. "And what of the places he has been visiting of late? Why, only last evening, I was told that Lord Lothian had seen the Duke of Yarmouth entering a house of disrepute on Thursday of last week!"

"That is a lie."

Lady Brackensill laughed shrilly, as though she had finally hit upon the truth and was now determined to cling to it. "Of course you would say so, Your Grace!"

"It *is* a lie, and I shall stand here and say it again to any who would hear it," the Duke said again, and as Louisa glanced up at him, she saw the sweat which was now beading across his forehead, the whiteness of his cheeks and the slight widening of his eyes… and her heart twisted.

"He was in my company that evening."

Lady Brackensill's dark smile fixed to her face, her confidence fading as her shoulders slumped. "I beg your pardon?"

"Thursday evening, I was in the Duke's company. Is that not so, Your Grace?" It was not the truth, of course, for she and her sisters had spent a quiet evening at home but all the same, the urge to protect the Duke from this rumor remained strong.

The Duke swallowed, glancing at her before he nodded. "Indeed. We had a private dinner, along with her sisters and my mother."

"Your mother who is leaving your house to reside elsewhere?" Lady Brackensill's smile returned, though it was an ugly one. "I have heard that she is to remove herself to another townhouse because she cannot stand being in your company!"

Louisa clicked her tongue. "Goodness, it does seem to me as though a great many rumours have been circling about the Duke of Yarmouth, does it not? I do wonder why they have come about with such fervency now that he has determined to alter his character. That seems rather strange to me, does it not to you, Lady Brackensill?" She continued on without pausing for breath, not giving the lady a chance to answer. "In addition, it will be highly embarrassing for those who spread these rumours when it is made clear that they speak nothing but falsehoods, will it not? I have already seen Lord Huntly shamed when he repeated the story that the Duke of Yarmouth had very little fortune left only to be informed that it was nothing but a lie. I do hope that not too many others will feel the heavy hand of shame and embarrassment settling upon them in that regard."

At this, Lady Brackensill's face flushed hot though she did not give an immediate response. Instead, she stuck out her chin, her eyes flashing, before turning and making her way back through the crowd, leaving the Duke and Louisa watching after her.

"Except," the Duke muttered, dropping his head, "my mother *is* intending to make her way from my townhouse and reside with a friend. That much is true, as well you know."

Louisa nodded slowly, her gaze still fixed upon Lady Brackensill though the crowd soon swallowed her up. "I am aware of that. I wonder if..." Licking her lips, she lifted her shoulders in a small shrug. "We must speak to your mother regardless, given that I have said we were all in company with you on Thursday evening. Might I...well, if you would permit me, might I speak with her privately?"

The Duke's eyes narrowed for just a moment though he then looked away. "If you wish to speak frankly about me to my mother, I cannot and will not protest."

"Then might we go in search of her?" Louisa asked, seeing that Ruth was now also engaged in conversation. "Both of my sisters are to take to the floor to dance, I think, so there is opportunity. I will tell them both to return to me thereafter."

There was another, momentary hesitation, only for the Duke then to nod. "Indeed, certainly. Let us go in search of her now and you will be able to say all that you need to, without my company."

Louisa smiled at him but he did not respond, his eyes holding a heaviness which, after a moment, she took to be genuine. Goodness, this gentleman truly had altered himself significantly, given that he would never have responded in such a way before! He would be doing all that he could to upset her, to push her away from him but now, he was willing to accommodate her, to permit her to do as she wished and was doing nothing to attempt to injure her in any way. Speaking briefly to each sister, she then took the

Duke's arm and allowed him to lead her through the crowd, quite sure that what she had to say to the Duchess would change a great deal for them all.

***

"Might I be frank?"

The Duchess nodded, her gaze pulling from Louisa and going to her son, who was standing a short distance away, leaning against the wall rather than stepping out into the crowd. The surprise in her expression did not fade as she returned her attention to Louisa, though Louisa was glad to see it.

"The rumours about your son are detrimental, not just to him but also to myself, as his betrothed," Louisa continued, quietly. "The one we have just told you about, the one we are now claiming as false and stating that we were with the Duke on Thursday evening, that is only one of them. There will be others, I am sure, for to my mind, it seems as though someone is speaking poorly of him purposefully."

The Duchess nodded, her lips pulling flat. "That should not come as a surprise to us, I am afraid."

"I quite understand." Wincing gently, Louisa lifted her shoulders. "The Duke does not have a good reputation and it is clear that he has injured a good many people by his actions. However, I must tell you that I have begun to believe that he is genuine in his desire to change."

At this, the Duchess' eyebrows flew up high, her eyes rounding.

"It may come a surprise to hear me speak so, but it is the truth. I must confess, while my acquaintance with the Duke may not be as intimate as yours, there exists within me a lingering hesitation, a sense of doubt and uncertainty that holds me back."

"I am surprised to hear you say such a thing," the Duchess said in reply, her eyes searching Louisa's face. "I would have thought…" She shook her head. "Ah, it does not matter what I think. The truth is, I believed that you would be a good match for my son because of your forthright manner and your determination, which I now see demonstrated in you, though not in the way I expected."

Louisa smiled. "The Duke could easily have broken off our betrothal, now that he knows you will not *encourage* him into another match." She emphasized the word, seeing the Duchess' rueful smile. "But he has not. He informs me that he wants to change his character, that he will become a better gentleman and I am slowly beginning to believe him."

The Duchess' lips curved gently. "I am most pleased to hear it; however, like yourself, I must confess to feeling a modicum of skepticism still."

Taking in a breath, Louisa spoke with as much boldness as she could, while making certain she was just as respectful as she ought to be. "Please, Your Grace, would you consider remaining in the house with the Duke?"

"I confess that I have been reconsidering my plans, though I have not yet shared anything like that with my son." The Duchess did not sound in the least bit upset but she did seem surprised, her eyes flickering with questions. "Is there a reason that you asked me?"

Louisa nodded, a little relieved that the Duchess did not appear to be angry with her for her bold question. "The fact is that Lady Brackensill spoke to both the Duke and myself about your plans and it now seems as though this is the next rumour that will be going through London! Though it is the only one with basis in truth."

The Duchess tilted her head just a little. "Might I ask if this means that you believe my son did *not* enter a house of disrepute? I know that you said to Lady Brackensill that we all took dinner together but that does not mean that he did not do as has been rumoured."

"I –" Louisa opened her mouth and then closed it again, frowning. She had, for whatever reason, instantly believed that the Duke had *not* done such a thing. Why did she believe that? There was nothing about him that suggested she ought to do so and yet her heart appeared to be softening towards him – softening so much that she *did* accept his word that he had not done so.

The Duchess smiled suddenly. "I will not push you for an answer, Lady Louisa. Thank you for your courage and your frankness in speaking to me. I will reconsider my plans to remove from the Duke's townhouse. In truth, I do not want to make things any more difficult for you than they already are, and I am aware that by removing from his house to another, I would only bring the ton's scrutiny all the more upon my son and yourself." Reaching out, she took Louisa's hand and then squeezed it tightly. "Thank you, Lady Louisa. Let me have a moment with my son and then I will leave you both in peace."

Louisa nodded, watching as the Duchess walked across the room to where the Duke stood. He straightened at once upon seeing her, inclining his head just a little to hear her speak. After a moment or two, his eyes sought hers and Louisa caught her breath at the sudden intensity she saw there, uncertain as what it was the Duchess was saying or what the Duke was thinking. He nodded, smiled and then kissed his mother's cheek before the Duchess stepped away. When he began to approach her, Louisa found her own heart beginning to pound with a sudden anticipation, though she could not understand where it came from. She was not drawn to the Duke of Yarmouth, was she? Yes, they were betrothed but that did not mean that she had any sort of genuine interest in him. At the moment, all she was doing was for the protection of herself and her own reputation, was it not?

"I thank you." The Duke not only bowed to her but then caught her hand, bowing the second time over it. "Whatever you have said to my mother, it appears that she now no longer intends to remove from the house. That rumour, it seems, will also be quashed." His lips brushed the back of her hand and Louisa's breath hitched, his nearness seeming to spark something in her. "I do not deserve such kindness nor such consideration, either from yourself or from my mother but I am very grateful for it."

Louisa could not speak for fear that the emotion which presently ran wild through her would evidence itself in her voice. The Duke, however, only smiled and then took a step back, though his hand still held hers.

"Now, might I ask you to dance, Lady Louisa? I should like to prove myself to you in this. I will not step away from you, will do nothing other than what every gentleman ought to do, I promise you."

Giving him a small nod, Louisa managed to smile as he set her hand on his arm before turning to walk to the center of the ballroom. Something had changed between them, she could feel it, but as yet, she could not be entirely certain as to what it was. It was both exhilarating and frightening and Louisa, as she made her way to the dance floor, let herself glance up at the Duke in question... but no answers were given to either her heart or her mind.

Chapter Fifteen

You do not know what you possess in having Lady Louisa.

The words his mother had said to him rang round and around Joseph's mind as he sat alone in the drawing room. He had not been entirely certain as to what Lady Louisa had said to his mother but whatever it had been, it had been enough to convince her to remain in his townhouse rather than going to stay elsewhere. That was something that had brought Joseph so much relief and joy that he had been unable to keep that from her, telling his mother how glad he was that she had reconsidered. She had then said those words to him and Joseph, kissing her cheek, had found himself agreeing.

Quite what that meant for him, however, he did not know. To find himself appreciative of the lady was one thing but to know that there was something between them now was quite another. He could not define it but the way that she smiled at him a little more easily, the way that they had danced together, saying nothing but looking into each other's eyes, and the way that she had come to his defense spoke of a change.

Joseph could only pray that it would grow in strength. Hearing the scratch at the door, he called for the butler to enter, his eyebrow lifting in question.

"Lord Quillon has come to call, Your Grace."

Joseph scrambled to his feet, his eyes widening. "Lord Quillon?"

"Yes, Your Grace."

"Send him in at once!" Joseph exclaimed, a little surprised to hear that his former friend had come to call, though grateful that he had. He curled up his fingers and then uncurled them again, tensing and then relaxing as he bounced on his toes for just a moment.

Lord Quillon walked in.

"Good afternoon, Yarmouth." Lord Quillon bowed quickly. "If you do not wish for me to remain in your company, then I do not need to do so. I can take my leave just as easily."

"No, no, please!" Joseph gestured to a chair. "Would you like a drink?"

Lord Quillon nodded and then settled himself in the chair Joseph had suggested. "Brandy, if you please."

"Of course." Joseph poured two small measures and then handed one to Lord Quillon before he himself sat opposite. He blinked quickly, trying not to let any other words escape him as he waited for his friend to speak.

"You are wondering why I am here, I suppose." Lord Quillon paused to take a sip of brandy as Joseph nodded, clutching the glass in his hands. "Well, I have heard some things about you of late and yet, at the same time, I have heard them refuted. I suppose I am here to try and ascertain what is true and what is false."

Joseph frowned. "Why should you wish to do that?"

"Because," Lord Quillon said, clearly, "if you are who the *ton* says you are, then I do not think that we can even be acquaintances. However, if you are as Lady Louisa says you are, then I might have to reconsider the ending of our friendship."

"Lady Louisa has been very kind in her defense of me," Joseph answered as Lord Quillon frowned. "As you know, however, my mother *did* think to remove herself from this house though that has now changed."

Faint surprise etched itself into Lord Quillon's expression.

"Again, that was due to Lady Louisa and her words to my mother," Joseph continued, "for it was she who convinced her to remain."

"I see." Lord Quillon's frown returned. "But I have heard two other rumours and yet I have heard them both refuted – by Lady Louisa, of course. I do not know whether they are true and she is only saying so in order to keep herself defended from the rumours of the *ton*, or because she is being truthful."

Joseph hesitated. "Might she be both?"

The frown on Lord Quillon's face grew heavier. "I do not understand"

"She is a great defender of me. She does so in order to protect her reputation, I am sure, but she is also speaking the truth, whether she realises it or not. On the 1st matter, which I presume is the rumour that I have lost my fortune, I proved to her that it was entirely untrue, and I can do so for you also, should you wish it." Clearing his throat, Joseph sat the little further forward in his chair. "When it comes to the matter of my so-called visitations to houses of disrepute, I can also assure you that it is entirely false, though I have no way of proving that."

"I see" Lord Quillon shook his head a little. "It is said that you were taking a private dinner with her on the night you were supposedly visiting these houses of ill reputation. I presume that is not entirely true."

Joseph nodded silently, praying that his friend would believe him, even though he knew that Lord Quillon had no reason to do so. "I was not in the house of disrepute, nor was I at dinner with Lady Louisa and her family. I was here." Gesturing to the room, Joseph offered a rueful smile. "I was here alone. I had no intention of going out to be in company and I had no desire to do so either. I am afraid that recognising who I truly am and how society sees me has resulted in a lack of inclination towards being a part of the *beau monde.*"

Taking another sip of his brandy, Lord Quillon tilted his head. "This is all very peculiar. Interesting, certainly, but peculiar all the same. I feel as though I do not know you, though I believe I began to feel that way the very moment I returned from my Great Adventure and was in your company once more."

A small, sad chuckle run through Joseph's frame. "Would you be surprised to know that I feel the very same way?"

Lord Quillon's eyebrows lifted.

"Ever since I realised how society views me and saw how little my friends and family wished to be in my company, the less I have known myself. I have not often thought of myself in dark or disagreeable terms, but I was forced to see the shadow that my character passes over everyone who comes into my company." He ran one hand over his chin. "And now I have a young lady who, despite the fact that I have been cruel to her, despite the fact that I have attempted to push her away, seems determined to make herself my defense. My mother told me that I did not realise what I had in her, and I must say I quite agree. There is a lot about myself that I am ashamed of. There is much about my character that I do not like and yet somehow I have Lady Louisa determined to stand by my side regardless." He shook his head. "Believe me when I say I do not know myself. I am trying to become someone that I have never known before, trying to be the gentleman that I ought to have always been. With all that being said, however, I am not certain that I will be able to do so."

It took some moments for Lord Quillon to answer and given the play of emotions across his features, Joseph was not at all sure whether or not his friend would believe him. He looked away, sipping his brandy as he waited, his stomach twisting.

"Goodness."

Joseph's gaze shot back towards Lord Quillon.

"I have never heard you speak in such a way before." Lord Quillon frowned, rubbing one hand over his chin in a thoughtful manner. "I did not think that my friendship meant all that much to you!"

Wincing, Joseph closed his eyes. "Yet another failing of mine, I am afraid."

"Though I do not mean it badly," his friend continued, quickly. "Indeed, I confess that I am rather impressed to know that my retreat from our friendship was enough to have you reconsidering yourself in such a strong light!"

"It was." Joseph threw back the rest of his brandy. "Quillon, I am truly sorry for my lack of consideration when it came to your advice and your thoughts on my behaviour. I apologise for my arrogance, for my selfishness, for my complete lack of willingness to even *think* about what it was that you had to say. It was wrong of me and I apologise for it."

Lord Quillon blinked then, after a moment, smiled albeit rather tentatively. "Does this mean that I might have to reconsider what I said about our friendship?"

Joseph could not help but laugh, shaking his head a little. "That is not something I can advise upon, that must be your decision alone. Whatever you decide, however, I will understand. After all, it has taken Lady Louisa some time to consider whether or not she fully believes me – and I am not certain that she has any sort of trust in me as yet – and I cannot fault her nor blame her for that. I feel the very same way about you."

"I see." Lord Quillon finished his brandy, then held out his glass. "Might I charge you for another?"

Joseph nodded at once, getting to his feet and feeling the last lingering tension strains between Lord Quillon and himself fade away. "Of course."

"I know you better than Lady Louisa."

"Yes, you do."

Lord Quillon took the glass of brandy from Joseph with a nod. "And that is why I believe your words. I do not doubt for a moment that you mean all that you say – and I believe it because you have never spoken in that way before. It is truly remarkable, I must say, and it brings me great pleasure to witness it. In brief, I believe it shall enhance your character most admirably. And is that not the very essence of our aspiration?"

Joseph nodded, struggling to speak for a few moments. His friend had returned in friendship to him, it seemed, and Joseph felt himself more than a little unworthy of it. "You have always been an upstanding fellow."

At this, Lord Quillon scoffed loudly, his eyes twinkling. "I hardly think so! You know as well as I that before I went on my Great Adventure, I had every intention of behaving just as I pleased – and indeed, I think that I did just as I wanted for some time! It was when I was *on* that Great Adventure, and when I became ill, that I realised how much I had to change."

"You and I were both a little roguish, I suppose, but I have become something else entirely." Joseph sat back down heavily, his shoulders rounding. "I have become a scoundrel with such a dreadful reputation, none in the *ton* wish to be in my company despite the fact I have such a high title!"

Lord Quillon smiled rather ruefully. "Sometimes the consequences of our actions are not always immediately apparent, I suppose."

"Indeed not."

"Though you have Lady Louisa now, do you not? A remarkable creature, I must say, given all that she has endured thus far – and I do not mean solely her betrothal to you."

Joseph looked back at him. "You mean her father and the responsibility he has set on her shoulders?"

Lord Quillon nodded. "A responsibility he should be taking on himself! I have not told you, I suppose, but I am now courting Lady Julia. She is dear friends with Lady Louisa and has told me everything about the present situation. It does seem to be very unfair, I must say. Why would he insist that she take on the role of chaperone for her sisters when she herself was not wed? Why was he quite contented to let *her* be the one without a match, to become a spinster, rather than take on his own duty and make certain all of his daughters found a match?"

"I do not know." A little surprised to hear that Lord Quillon was now courting, Joseph smiled. "I am pleased to hear that you have found someone to pursue, however. I know that this is what you have long desired."

Lord Quillon's smile was gentle, his expression warm. "Lady Julia is quite wonderful. Ever since I first set eyes on her, I have found myself caught up with nothing but thoughts of her, of her smile, of her company, of her heart. I want to *win* her heart, you understand, rather than this simply being a match of suitability."

"A love match."

"Precisely." Lord Quillon let out a small, contented sigh. "Our courtship is blossoming and I am all the more delighted with her every time I see her."

Recognizing something of what Lord Quillon said was within his own heart also, Joseph frowned and then took a sip of his brandy.

"You are displeased to hear me say such a thing?"

"No, no, not at all!" Setting his brandy down, Joseph rose to his feet, gesticulating as he spoke, his words coming out quickly for fear that he might damage their renewed friendship. "Forgive me, I did not mean to give the impression that I found anything upsetting or disagreeable in what you said. It is only that... well, I find myself recognising some of what you have said."

Lord Quillon's face suddenly split with a smile. "You mean to say that you are feeling some great emotion for the lady?"

Joseph shook his head quickly. "No, I would not say that there was any great emotion. Instead, I have found myself thinking of her a little more, being *drawn* to her company, as you have said. I do not know if that means anything or if there is some great emotion that will soon come with it but it is certainly... interesting to consider."

An eyebrow lifted. "You are aware that you might well be growing fond of the lady?"

Joseph opened his mouth to say that no, he had no thought of that, only to close his mouth again slowly. He did not want to do as he had always done and refute what his friend had said in place of making himself out to be correct. "You know more about these things than I. I confess that my first urge is to refute you but I will not."

Lord Quillon chuckled, his eyes dancing. "Now I know that you are just as you have said in your desire to change, for no Duke of Yarmouth that I know would ever have admitted to that!"

Chuckling a little wryly, Joseph shrugged. "I am altering myself entirely, it seems... even down to my very heart."

Chapter Sixteen

"You are courting?"

Lady Julia nodded, her eyes alight with evident happiness. "I am. He asked me after having already spoken to my father."

Louisa's eyes widened. "He spoke to your father about his intentions? Already?"

Laughing, Julia slipped her hand through Louisa's arm as they walked through the London streets. "Yes, indeed. It seems that he wants to make himself quite clear, both to my father and to myself. I am grateful for that."

"And you are contented with him?"

Lady Julia nodded. "Yes, more than contented, if I am to be truthful." The gentle smile on her face made Louisa's heart squeeze with happiness for her friend, truly glad that she had found someone so wonderful.

"I do hope that I will be asked to be a bridesmaid," she said, making her friend laugh delightedly. "You know I will be upset if I am not asked."

"Of course I shall ask you, though you must not hope for too much too soon... though I think I am speaking to myself rather than to you when I say such things!"

Louisa smiled. "You care for him?"

"I do." Lady Julia sighed, her smile still stretched across her face. "I think him wonderful. He is kind-hearted, considerate, gentle in nature and yet determined to do all that he ought when it comes to our courtship. We have taken tea together many a time, he has come to dinner and we have gone to dine with him. There have been many walks, dances and conversations and all of them have become a little better than the times before! And, of course, I think him *very* handsome."

Giggling, Louisa elbowed her friend gently. "How could you not?" For a moment, a picture of the Duke filled her mind and Louisa's smile began to fade, wondering as to why she was beginning to think of him when they were talking about Lord Quillon.

"The Duke is handsome also."

Louisa snatched in a breath, her eyes widening as she looked at her friend. "I beg your pardon?"

"You heard what I said," Lady Julia answered, a twinkle in her eye. "The *ton* has always said that the Duke of Yarmouth is a handsome fellow so it would not be surprising for *you* to think so also."

"Oh." Louisa shrugged but turned her gaze away. "Of course he is."

"And might I ask if your opinion of him has improved at all of late? I have heard the rumours, of course, but I have also heard that each one has been refuted. I think that, at this moment, society does not know what to make of your Duke!"

Louisa hesitated, looking away from her friend and towards the shops which lined the streets, trying to think of what would be best to say. "The truth is, Julia, not all of the rumours are true." She looked back at her friend, seeing a light frown pull across Julia's face. "There is one that I am uncertain about – the rumour that he was at a house of disrepute – but the Duke says that it is not the truth and thus, I have decided to believe him. More than that," she admitted, wincing just a little, "I have told the *ton* that I was present with him so that it could certainly not be true, though that in itself was a lie."

"You are defending him?" Blinking in surprise, Lady Julia's eyes widened. "Why would you do that?"

"Because," Louisa admitted, a little heavily, "I have come to think a little better of him than I did before. When he tells me that one rumour is a lie, then I am more inclined to believe him and, therefore, I find my heart eager to defend him. Yes, there is some self preservation there also given that I do not want the *ton* to think poorly of me, for my own reputation could also be damaged, but that is not the main purpose behind my defense of him."

"Goodness!" Lady Julia shook her head quickly, as though trying to remove the expression of surprise from her face, perhaps seeing how Louisa was upset by it. "Forgive me, I do not mean to judge you in any way, I assure you! It is only a little surprising to hear you say such a thing about him. Though, perhaps, that is a good thing! It is good that you will not be at odds with your husband, once you are wed. If there is some good in him that you can cling to, then I am glad for you."

"He still insists that he wants to change, that he wants to become the gentleman he knows he ought to be," Louisa said, speaking slowly as her brows furrowed lightly. "As I have said, I am more inclined to believe him, though I am still not certain. He certainly appears to have altered somewhat already."

"Though you cannot be certain that he did *not* go to the house of disrepute."

Louisa looked at her friend, her own frown still present. "It is very strange, is it not? When he said that it was a lie, my heart believed him. In a single instant, without even considering anything else, I trusted that he spoke the truth. I do not know what it was, something about how he looked, something in his eyes which told me that he was being honest. And yet, my heart says I cannot trust him fully."

For some moments, Lady Julia said nothing. Then, after a small sigh, she lifted her shoulders lightly and then let them fall. "I do not know what to say. Your heart is your own, your considerations your own.

Louisa pulled her gaze away from her friend, having been silently hoping that Lady Julia would be encouraging.

"Lord Quillon told me that he was going to call upon the Duke this afternoon," Lady Julia continued, making Louisa's gaze rush back towards her. "He did not say as to why he wished to speak to him but he only said that he had much to think about."

"Do you think that he too might be willing to reconsider his friendship with the Duke? Might he too be feeling much the same way as I do?"

Julia smiled and then patted Louisa's hand. "Who can say? It may be that or it may be that he wishes to express some harshness over some matter or other though, given what *you* have said, I do wonder if it is the former." She took in a deep breath as a trickle of excitement began to wind through Louisa's heart. "Perhaps this Duke of Yarmouth will become a trustworthy gentleman after all."

***

"Are you quite ready?"

Louisa nodded, having purchased two new books from the bookshop. "I am. Do you wish to take a hackney or will we walk back to your townhouse? I can take the hackney from there."

"Or I will send you in the carriage," Lady Julia answered, with a smile as she held open the bookshop door so they might both step outside. "Yes, I am content to walk, though Mama will, no doubt, screech that I have been out for so long and that I will have no time to prepare for the ball this evening!"

Louisa laughed. "I am sure that Lord Quillon will think you quite beautiful no matter what you look like," she said, only for a few squeals of laughter to ring out, catching her attention. Looking ahead, she saw a small group of ladies all standing together, with two gentlemen now ambling towards them, flickers of interest in their eyes. Louisa shrugged inwardly and made to continue her conversation with Lady Julia, only for her to hear her own name being spoken.

"I do feel sorry for Lady Louisa, for she has no choice in the matter! Her father has agreed to it and thus, what can she do but marry him?"

A slow heat began to build in Louisa's chest, rising up to her neck and into her cheeks.

"Wait." Lady Julia caught her arm. "We should not walk past them. Come, let us go another way and – "

"No." Louisa shook off her friend's hand. "I have already been fighting rumours about the Duke himself. I will not let anyone else speak of me in such a way, not when I am close enough to hear it!" Despite her embarrassment, she lifted her chin and approached the group of ladies, some of whom caught their breath at the sight of her, their smiles instantly fading.

"I should like to inform you all that my father did not force me into this betrothal," she said clearly, as everyone in the group looked back at her, including the two gentlemen who had come to join them. "I should also prefer it if you did not speak such nonsense to any other; there have been enough rumours at present about the Duke of Yarmouth and I certainly do not wish for there to be any other!" Her face hot, she set her gaze to each and every face, feeling her stomach twisting inwardly as she fought to keep her composure. She wanted to appear strong and determined, not wishing to show any sign of weakness for fear that the ladies present would pounce upon it – and make yet more rumours spring from that.

"Forgive us, Lady Louisa." One of the young ladies – one that Louisa recognized – bobbed a quick curtsy. "We were only expressing our sympathy about your situation, that was all. There was no malice meant in it."

A few murmurs of agreement came from the others and Louisa nodded though she did not let the conversation go. "Be that as it may, it might be wise, then, to ascertain the truth before speaking about it in such a way, do you not think? It is true that I am betrothed to the Duke of Yarmouth. It is not true that I have been forced into it. Indeed, the Duke himself has told me that I may end our betrothal if I wish it and that he would take the responsibility for it!"

"And... and you do not wish to end it?" another of the ladies asked, sounding utterly astonished as Louisa's face grew hot, swallowing tightly as she pinned her gaze to the rather bold young lady.

"No, I do not."

"But why?" the lady asked again, staring at Louisa with wide eyes, as though she had never seen such an extraordinary creature before. "The Duke of Yarmouth does not have a good reputation, as I am sure you must be aware! Do you not know that most of society pities you? That we look upon you with sympathy?"

"Mary, please." Another young lady put a hand to the one speaking, though there was a slight glint in her eye which Louisa did not like. "You are being much too forward."

Louisa sensed the presence of Lady Julia beside her before she saw her, grateful for the way that her friend had come to join her, despite the fact that she clearly did not think this a wise idea. "While I appreciate that the *ton* feels sympathy towards me, I can assure you, it is entirely unnecessary. I am fully aware of the Duke's reputation but for reasons which are my own, I *will* marry him. I would very much appreciate it if there was as little as possible spoken about me, however, for hearing my name in rumours and whispers is not something I value."

"And," Lady Julia added, before the murmurings began, "might I also remind you all that you stand in the presence of the lady who will soon be the *Duchess* of Yarmouth?"

There came a few quiet gasps at this, as though some there had not realized the significance of this. Whatever they said and did now would be remembered and, given that Louisa *would* soon be the Duchess and hold a very high title indeed within society, it would not be wise to upset her. That was not something that Louisa had considered but seeing now how some of the ladies flushed and looked away from her in obvious embarrassment made her appreciate Lady Julia's presence and thoughtfulness all the more. It seemed that, with this reminder, she would be less likely to have the whispers of the *ton* floating around her.

"I shall take my leave of you now." With a nod to one or two, Louisa kept her head high and turned to walk away, Lady Julia following quickly after her. They said nothing for some moments, only for Louisa to let out a long, slow breath and then grin at her friend. "My dear Julia, I think you may have silenced a good many wagging tongues this afternoon!"

Her friend chuckled. "I am glad, for they have no need to speak of you in whispers! Though I must say, it did take me a little by surprise to have you speak with such determination. I think it will have astonished some of them also, though I do not think that it is a bad thing. It will, I think, have even less of them willing to talk about you in that way."

Louisa nodded, her heart lifting just a little as she found herself thinking of the Duke. "If I can quash more rumours about the Duke and about myself, then I think that an excellent thing," she said, softly. "I admit that I am quite determined about my marriage now. I must hope, however, that the Duke does prove himself to me, that his word *can* be trusted and that his character improves in the way that he has promised."

"I hope so too," Lady Julia answered, softly. "For your sake, I pray it will be just as you have said."

Chapter Seventeen

Yawning, Joseph stretched out his legs and crossed them at the ankle, glass in hand. He had enjoyed an early morning ride through the park, had returned to his townhouse to deal with matters of business and, thereafter, had taken yet another turn about the park though this time, it had been in the company of his betrothed. He and Lady Louisa had enjoyed a very pleasant afternoon walking together and, much to Joseph's surprise, he had not given a single moment's thought to what else he might be doing or whose company he might be missing out on. It was as though Lady Louisa now took up so much of his thoughts and his attention, he had nothing to offer anyone else.

Smiling to himself, Joseph leaned his head back in his chair and closed his eyes, silently thinking to himself just how much had changed. He had regained his friendship with Lord Quillon, his mother had chosen to remain in their townhouse rather than move to another place and though there were rumors abounding, he was able to fight them off without too much difficulty.

Though that is all thanks to Lady Louisa, he considered, his smile growing all the more. *Lady Louisa who has given me so much. She convinced my mother to remain. She has been defending the rumors. She has even lied for me in order to push back the whispers of the* ton. *I do not think I will ever find a way to show her how grateful I am for all of that.*

He swallowed, a slight frown replacing his smile.

Is there more to what I feel for her than mere gratitude? What if this mild affection is something more? Something even greater than I have ever permitted myself to imagine?

"I.. I do not know," he said aloud, speaking his own thoughts to himself. "Does it matter?"

Why should it matter, he considered, returning to his quiet thoughts again. If he had a gentle affection for the lady, then that was not something to be feared, something to turn from. Rather, he could acknowledge it but that was all. It would not grow, he was certain, for that was not something he had ever considered or expected for his future.

I am a little afraid of it.

That thought made Joseph frown. Why should he be afraid of his emotions? Getting to his feet, he strode across the room and poured himself a brandy, throwing it back in one gulp. A slight tremor ran through him and he frowned, trying to make sense of all that he was thinking and feeling. Why was it that the thought of having a growing and deepening affection for Lady Louisa made him recoil? Admittedly, he had always told himself that such things were foolishness and yes, he had vowed never to permit himself to be so, given how ridiculous he thought it, but did that mean that he thought the same now?

The frown on his forehead grew deeper. "I have no need for it," he told himself aloud, nodding as the thought settled in his mind, calming him. "I have no need for any thought of love nor of affection." Taking in a deep breath, he poured another measure of brandy but this time, let it swirl around the glass. "I do not think I shall ever let my heart twist in that direction." He nodded again, his frown lingering still. There was something about it all that frightened him, loathe though he was to admit it. It was as though, in considering that he might fall in love, he would find himself weak, foolish and his affection not returned. Closing his eyes, Joseph's shoulders dropped just a little. That was the crux of it, he realized. The thought of becoming vulnerable enough to confess that he had an affection for Lady Louisa, only to see her shake her head and tell him she had nothing of the same within her heart was a thought that shook him to the very core – and who was he to think that he might garner some tenderness from her? He would not be worthy of it, would not be offered it, he was sure! No, it was best to protect himself from that, to push aside all thought and consideration that urged him towards growing closer to her. That way, he would protect his own heart.

"Your Grace?"

Joseph turned, ready to bark at his butler for opening the door and interrupting him, only for the butler to step aside with an apologetic look on his face. Without warning, none other than the lady he had been considering rushed into the room, her eyes wide, one hand clutching a piece of paper.

"Forgive me, Yarmouth, but I could not wait! The butler knocked but you did not answer and – "

"You are dismissed." With a curt nod to the butler, Joseph looked down into Lady Louisa's wide eyes, his heart thudding with the awareness of how she had spoken to him, that informal manner which spoke of a closeness between them. "Whatever is the matter?"

"I am sorry for rushing in, but I could not wait! My father is not at home and thus, my sisters are waiting in the carriage, but I had to show you this. Look!" Her hand caught his arm as though she wanted to keep him close to her, the other hand lifting so that he could see what she held. Joseph took it from her carefully, forced to use both hands to unfold the letter, though, to his surprise, Lady Louisa stayed close, wrapping her hand around his arm and standing so near him, he caught the sweet scent of roses whispering towards him.

Joseph closed his eyes briefly, feeling a little off-balance as a wave of emotion threatened to crash over him, halted only by his own determination to stop these feelings crushing him. Clearing his throat, he forced his attention and his gaze upon the letter, steadfastly ignoring the desire to give in to what he felt. Reading the few lines, his eyes widened in surprise, a knot tying itself in his stomach. "When was this sent to you?"

"This afternoon, only half an hour ago," she answered, her eyes searching his face as he looked back at her. "I cannot understand it."

His lips pulling to one side, Joseph read the letter again, though this time, he spoke it out loud. "'Lady Louisa, I write as a friend, though you might not think me so. The Duke of Yarmouth is a scoundrel and you must not tie yourself to him, no matter the difficulties that might be brought to bear, should you break the betrothal. I will do what I can to encourage your father to break it on your behalf. I should hate to see you injured, as you no doubt shall be.'" As he read the final few words, Joseph's heart sank, his spirits dropping sharply. With a clearing of his throat, he folded up the letter, returned it to Lady Louisa and then shook his head as he stepped away from her. "They are quite correct, however."

"Correct?" Lady Louisa's breath caught in a gasp of shock,

her eyes widening, one hand pressed to her stomach. "What do you mean?"

Having no understanding of her sharp reaction to his words, Joseph shrugged lightly. "I will injure you, no doubt."

Lady Louisa began to blink rapidly, her eyes swimming with sudden tears. "But I thought... I thought that you had told me that you would change, that you were determined to do so. Why should you wish to injure me now?"

It was as though lightening had struck him. Seeing her close to tears and realizing what his foolish words had done, Joseph let out a small cry of exasperation at his own foolishness and, urgently, came back close to her.

"That is not what I meant, Louisa, I assure you." His hands found hers, clasping them both tightly, the letter falling to the floor. "Forgive me, forgive me for frightening you. No, I do not mean that I will do so deliberately, for every word that I have said to you as regards my desire to change has been quite true. I only meant that, given my reputation and the rumours which continually grow, I will inadvertently injure you, simply because you are connected to me in that way. I will, inevitably, cause you pain."

"Oh." Lady Louisa's blinking became a little less rapid, her breathing becoming slower as she understood his meaning. Her shoulders dropped, the tension in her frame lessened and after a few moments, she finally looked back up into his eyes. "I understand."

"I am sorry." A slight ache came into Joseph's heart as he realized just how quickly she had thought ill of him, how hurriedly her mind had turned to considering him poorly. "I should not have spoken so quickly and with such inconsideration, especially when I have such a dreadful reputation – and when your trust in me is not well established."

Lady Louisa took in another breath, her tears gone completely now. "It is growing, Your Grace."

A pang bruised his heart. "Call me Yarmouth, if you wish." The urge for her to do so, for him to hear that softness of expression upon her lips grew ferociously. "We do not need to be so formal, do we?"

For the first time since she had stepped into the room, a smile graced Lady Louisa's lips. "No, I suppose we do not... Yarmouth."

Joseph swallowed tightly, suddenly becoming very aware of just how close she was to him. The softness of her hands in his made heat tear up his arms, sending his heart into a rushed rhythm. The gentleness in her eyes made him want to linger in this moment, to continue gazing at her for as long as he could. He could not explain what it was that he felt, could not quite understand why he had such a longing for it was not something he had ever experienced before. Yes, he had often had the desire to pull a lady close into his arms, but he had never once thought about simply looking down into her eyes and remaining there! The desire to have her closer was present, certainly, but it was as if he did not want to hasten that moment, as though he could not bring himself to do such a thing yet.

What is happening to me?

Everything he had vowed only a few minutes before seemed to fade away to nothingness, like a cloud that dissipates into the wind. Lady Louisa had not moved either, he realized, as though she too felt much the same way as he. Joseph swallowed tightly as her fingers threaded through his, connecting them in an all the more intimate way.

"I am sorry that I doubted you so quickly."

Joseph shook his head no. "I will not have you apologise, Louisa. I fully understand why you did." His head dropped for a moment as the reminder of just how dark a character he had once possessed – and still tried to break through, at times – struck him. "I cannot promise that I will never injure you. Though I do say that I will do all that I can to prevent it."

"That is good enough for me."

Her voice was a whisper, forcing Joseph's gaze back towards her beautiful blue eyes, so clear and guileless. It was as though she were some sort of wonderful angel, pure and without fault, while he stood there in his rags and his shame, clinging to her desperately. His heart twisted and he shook his head. "I have been considering just how little I deserve you as my betrothed, Louisa. Even now, I see it. I know that there is much that I need to prove but to see you so afraid of my lack of good character shames me again. I do not like that you must fight against the rumours of the *ton*. It is a burden that I alone must bear and yet – "

"These are things we can bear together, are they not?" Lady Louisa took one of her hands from his and for a moment, Joseph thought that she meant to step back from him. Much to his astonishment, however, she placed a hand lightly upon his chest, her eyes looking up at him, searching gently.

"Together?" Joseph's voice was husky now, her gentle touch searing him through his clothes, sending his heart into a wild, furious rhythm as the urge to lower his head and kiss her began to wind through him. It was a familiar desire, one that he had felt – and given into – many a time, but this time, it gave him pause. Yes, he could easily do as he wished, yes he could kiss her, wrap his arms about her and pull her into his embrace, but something about that seemed tawdry. He had done such a thing with many a young lady but with Lady Louisa, it felt different. Was it that he did not truly wish to? Or that, this time, he was almost afraid to do so?

"I suppose," he said, clearing his throat gruffly and shattering the quiet expectation in the air between them, "we should also consider who might have sent you this letter and why they have done so."

Lady Louisa's gaze dropped immediately and she stepped away from him, leaving him with nothing but a sense of coldness which wrapped around his chest.

"Yes," she murmured, her hand now pulling away from his, ending the connection which had brought him so much confusion. "Yes, I suppose those are important questions to consider." She let out a laugh but it held no joy within it. Rather, it was dry and brittle. "That is, after all, why I came to speak with you in the first place."

He nodded. "Yes, I understand. Do you – " He hesitated, trying to remember what it was he had wanted to say, struggling now to bring himself out of the connection which he had just begun to shatter. "Do you have any thought as to who it might be?"

"How should I know?" There was a slight harshness to Lady Louisa's voice now, as though what he had done had pained her a great deal. "I bring this to you in the hope that you might know who it is. You are the one who has garnered so much upset from the *ton*, the one who has brought so much discontent to others. Surely it cannot be difficult to think of who it might be?"

"Because there would be so many?" Joseph asked, his jaw jutting forward as she gazed back at him, her own lips pulled tight. "Is that what you mean?"

Lady Louisa blinked, frowned, and then shook her head. "I – I did not mean to say that... that is, I do not mean to suggest... " Putting one hand to her forehead, she shook it again and then turned away from him. "Perhaps I should not have come."

She made to walk away from him and something poured into Joseph's heart, something that rent him apart. In one swift movement, he had not only caught her hand but had pulled her against him. He caught only a glimpse of her wide eyes as he lowered his head, kissing her in a way that he had never kissed anyone before.

He did not know what had come over him. All the questions over what he ought to be doing or ought not to be doing flew from him in that moment, his arms going tightly around her, his heart beating wildly as he slanted his head just a little, aware of how she had slowly begun to soften against him. Her shoulders dropped, her hands pressed lightly against his chest and her lips softened as he deepened the kiss, as though she too had been waiting for this moment.

You have fallen in love with her.

The thought struck him, hard, and Joseph snatched in a breath, breaking the kiss and stepping back from her as his hands fell to his sides. Lady Louisa's eyes were wide and fixed, her mouth a little ajar, her cheeks flushed as she stood stock still. Joseph did not move, his chest heaving, his hands curling tightly as he tried to find something to say, something to *do* rather than simply gazing back at her – but he could say nothing. This afternoon had been a tumultuous one, filled with all manner of confusing and unsettling thoughts which, he now realized, had ended in his heart practically dragging him towards her and wrapping her in his arms.

What was he to do now?

"Louisa, I – "

She closed her eyes, sniffed and then swallowed hard.

"I did not mean to."

Lady Louisa's eyes opened. "Did you want to?" Her voice was so quiet, it sounded like it was coming from very far away, making Joseph wince.

"No, that is not what I meant. I wanted to but I also did not. I was battling within myself and, unfortunately, I gave in."

Her eyes flared wide. "Unfortunately?" Her voice was strangled and Joseph winced, realizing what a mistake he had made.

"I am not managing to explain myself well, I am sorry. I – "

Lady Louisa shook her head. "I must take my leave. I should go. Do excuse me."

"Louisa, please, wait!" Joseph hurried forward but she was already gone, the door closing behind her and Joseph was, once again, left alone.

Letting out a groan, Joseph clapped one hand to his forehead, then threw his head back. Somehow, he had taken what might have been a wonderful moment and ruined it entirely by his lack of wisdom in what he had said. Letting out a heavy breath, he dropped his head, closed his eyes and groaned.

What a disastrous afternoon this had become… and all because he had been afraid to listen to what was truly being said by his heart.

Chapter Eighteen

He kissed me.

Louisa absently ran one finger across her lips, then, recognizing what she was doing, dropped her hand to her side. The kiss had been something she had not been able to forget. She had slept fitfully, recalling every moment of it, remembering everything she had felt and how happy she had been only for the realization of just how broken she had been thereafter.

When he had used the word, 'unfortunately', it had been as though part of her inside had turned to dust. Her heart, which had been filled with a mixture of both excitement and concern – concern that she was just one of many a young lady that he had kissed – had broken into pieces when he had said such a thing. Clearly, he had regretted their kiss while she had found herself captured by it, wondering as to what it was that it meant. It was obvious to her now that he had not meant to, had done so perhaps out of a sense of duty, knowing that it would soon come and be expected of him and wishing to take the opportunity to do so. He had regretted it, perhaps, because of her reaction, her obvious response to it and that had brought her all manner of shame and embarrassment. Her own heart, which had begun to feel various things for the gentleman, was now mortified that it had held onto those feelings, shamed that it had let them grow. No, it was time now for her to set aside such things, remind herself that she was to marry a reforming rogue and recognize that any sort of genuine affection for her was not likely to come about.

"You look upset."

Louisa started and then tried to smile as Lady Julia came to stand beside her. "Good evening, Julia. No, I am not upset. Only thoughtful."

"Why might that be?"

Louisa's smile grew a little wry and she shook her head. "There are various reasons, but the first is to tell you that I received a letter from someone yesterday, informing me that they were going to do all they could to make certain that my father ended my betrothal to the Duke of Yarmouth."

"What?" Lady Julia's voice was a little louder than Louisa had expected, and she shushed her friend quietly, though Lady Julia did nothing to moderate her voice. "You mean to say that someone is determined to *end* your betrothal to the Duke for their own reasons? Do you think that they wish to marry him themselves?"

Louisa let out a quiet, broken laugh and shook her head. "No, not given what was said. It was clear that the letter writer knows the Duke of Yarmouth and his reputation. It appears to me as though they are doing what they can to protect me, as though forcing my father to end the betrothal is a good thing."

"And you no longer believe that it would be."

"No." Louisa frowned as she said this, her heart quickening. "I suppose… goodness, Julia, I confess I do not know what to think!"

Lady Julia's eyebrow lifted gently.

"He… he kissed me," Louisa stammered, her face growing hot as she kept her voice quiet. "It was the most wonderful and the most painful thing in all of the world, however, for he told me that he regretted it."

Her friend's eyes rounded. "Whatever did he mean by that?"

"I do not know." Louisa let out a small sigh. "His words were that he did wish to kiss me but that he also did not wish to do so, and that, in the end, he *unfortunately* gave in."

Lady Julia frowned. "That is a strange thing to say." When she said nothing further, Louisa tilted her head, waiting for the explanation. "By that, I mean to say that it is unusual for that gentleman to say that he was battling within himself over whether he ought to kiss you or not. I would have thought that he would have been determined to do so and would have thought nothing of it! After all, he has wrapped his arms around many a lady, I am sure." She smiled gently at Louisa. "So why would he be battling the thought of kissing you?"

"I do not know. I had not thought of that." Louisa's lips twisted for a moment as her gaze roved around the ballroom, not stopping on anything or anyone specifically. "I only heard him say that he regretted it and since then, I have been rather upset about it all."

The edges of Lady Julia's lips turned upwards. "Why would that be? Why are you upset?"

Louisa opened her mouth to answer, only to snap it closed again. Seeing the glint in her friend's eye, she looked away, heat beginning to climb up into her face. "I do not like the thought that he regretted kissing me."

"Because you did not regret it? Because you felt the connection between you blossom and because your heart holds an affection for him?"

Swallowing tightly, Louisa looked back at her friend. "Would it be dreadful if I admitted that all to be true?"

"Dreadful?" Her friend laughed and shook her head. "No, of course not! Why would it be so?"

"Because it is foolish! Foolish to think myself drawn to a Duke who does not truly want to kiss me, who will not, no doubt, ever have any true affection for me! Why should I let my heart feel something for him when I know that he is not going to return such feelings?"

"Do you think you can be sure of that?" Lady Julia's voice had softened. "He says that he is changing, that he is determined to alter himself. What if his heart will change with it? What if he truly does begin to fall in love with you, just as you have with him?"

Louisa opened her mouth to protest that she was not falling in love with him but then closed it again, being interrupted by the arrival of Lord Quillon. He beamed at them both, though Louisa saw that his attention was pulled firmly towards Lady Julia, finding her heart aching just a little as she longed for the very same thing to be in her own life – albeit to see it in the eyes of Lord Yarmouth.

"How delightful to see you both this evening!" he exclaimed, bowing low. "I do hope that both of you will be dancing, though you will forgive me if I take Lady Julia's waltz, Lady Louisa?"

"Of course I do."

"Which is just as well given that I would like to step out with the lady for the waltz."

Something heavy dropped into Julia's stomach as she turned to see the Duke of Yarmouth bowing low, having neither seen nor heard him approaching. "You – you wish to dance the waltz with me?"

"I do." A hint of a smile touched his lips, though it did not linger. "That is, if you would wish to dance with me? I will not force it upon you."

In answer, Louisa slipped off her dance card from her wrist and held it out to him, aware that it would be most improper for her to refuse. She had no reason to do so, especially not when the gentleman was her betrothed!

"Ah, I can see that Rachel and Ruth are being brought back to me," she said, breaking the silence which had come down upon the four of them ,with both the gentlemen bowing their heads over the dance cards. "They were dancing the quadrille, you see."

She glanced to Lady Julia, feeling herself tense and awkward, though her friend only smiled but with a twinkle in her eye. There was no reason for what she was saying but yet, she was speaking regardless, the strain running through her making her whole body hum.

"Good evening, Your Grace." Ruth was the first one to greet them, smiling warmly. "Lord Quillon, good evening. And to you also, Julia!" When her gaze turned to Louisa, however, the smile faded. "Louisa, might I – "

"Good evening to you all! I do hope that you will dance with us also, Lord Quillon, though I understand that your attention will be firmly fixed to Lady Julia!" Rachel laughed but Louisa winced inwardly at her sister's forwardness, though Lord Quillon did not seem to mind in the least.

"I would be glad to sign your dance cards also," the Duke added but much to Louisa's horror, Rachel quickly shook her head and pulled her dance card back from where she had held it out to Lord Quillon, as though afraid that the Duke would snatch it.

"No, I thank you." She said nothing more, gave no further explanation but instead, merely smiled briefly but then turned her attention to Lord Quillon. Louisa watched as the Duke's eyebrows lifted, his gaze moving to Ruth though she did not say a single word. Instead, she moved to stand by Louisa, her hand going to her arm.

"Louisa, might I speak with you for a moment?"

Louisa nodded. "Of course. What is the matter?"

Her sister shook her head. "Not here. Privately."

A heaviness sank into Louisa's bones at the weight of seriousness in Ruth's eyes. "What has happened?" Taking Ruth by the elbow, she turned them both away from the small group, knowing that Julia would wait with Rachel until they returned. "Is there something wrong?"

Ruth looked back at her, coming around to face Louisa as they stood to the back of the ballroom. "It is another rumour, my dear sister. Though this time, it is a difficult one indeed for me not only to hear but to also tell you."

Louisa tried to shrug, tried to pretend that it did not matter to her, though she could not keep the worry from her voice. "You must tell me, Ruth. You cannot keep this from me. I must tell the Duke also."

"He may already be aware of it." The moment those words were said, Ruth dropped her head, redness in her cheeks. "Forgive me, I did not mean to suggest that he has done as is whispered. I know that there have been many rumours and they have been proved to be false and I suppose this one might also be, though it appears a little more unlikely."

Every word pierced Louisa like a heated iron, scraping across her skin. "Pray, Ruth, enlighten me, I beseech you."

***

Her sister took in a deep breath, then reached to take Louisa's hands. "There is a lady by the name of Lady Clement. Her husband, they think, was taken by the sea when he went to visit the continent last summer. She is saying that the Duke of Yarmouth kept her company one evening last week... and that he did not leave her house until the following morning."

Louisa swallowed hard, a chill wrapping around her. She did not respond, trying to let the words sink into her heart and doing her utmost to fight against them, to tell herself that they could not – ought not, at the very least – to be believed.

"Are you all right?" Ruth's eyes were searching hers but Louisa only turned away, dullness beginning to wash over her.

"Louisa, I did not mean to injure you! I thought it important to tell you."

"I understand."

I will inevitably cause you pain. The words the Duke had spoken to her only the day before came back in a rush and tears quickly stung her eyes. Closing them so that the flood would not lead to weeping, Louisa took in short, quick breaths as she battled the swell of upset, refusing to let a single tear fall. She heard Ruth speaking to her, heard her voice but could not make out the words. Blood was roaring in her ears, her thoughts were flooding through her and it felt as though all of the world was swirling around her, threatening to drag her to the very depths.

"*There* you are!"

A sharp, shrill voice rang and seemed to bring everything into perfect clarity. Louisa opened her eyes, turning to see a lady hurrying towards the Duke of Yarmouth, who stood stock still, his eyes fixed to her and what appeared to be a look of horror beginning to pull into his expression.

"I am sorry, Yarmouth, but I had no choice but to tell them all."

"Tell them all what?" the Duke replied, his gaze darting one between the lady and to Louisa, who had made her way back to join them. "I do not know what you speak of, Lady Clement."

Lady Clement? Shock rifled through Louisa's heart and she suddenly could not move, could not take another step or even turn her head to look at the lady. She saw Rachel's lip curl with disgust, making it clear to Louisa as to why she had refused to dance with the Duke. Louisa closed her eyes tightly again, her hands tight, fingernails painfully pressing into her palms. What was the lady to say of this?

"You remained at my townhouse all through the night and into the day," Lady Clement said, in almost a sing song voice. "I will not – cannot – let you go! Even though you are to wed, I have tell the *ton* about our connection in the hope that you will not abandon me! We have such a sweetness in our time together, time which I cannot simply forget about."

"This is nonsense." The tight, rasping voice of the Duke forced Louisa's eyes open, seeing the Duke standing rigid, his face white but his eyes narrowed. "I have not seen you in months! I will admit that we have often spent time – long periods of time – together but that does not mean that I have done so recently!"

"How can you pretend so?" Lady Clement put one hand to her forehead, blinking quickly as though to hide tears. "You break me with your sharp words. I understand that you are to be wed soon but can you not see that my heart cries out in agony over this, knowing that you will be set aside from me forever?" A glint came into her eye that made Louisa's blood go cold. "That is, unless you intend to continue on as you are, even once you are wed? In which case, I ought not to have said anything!"

Louisa did not know where to look, her stomach twisting this way and that, her skin going from hot to cold and back again. She was breathing quickly, her chest growing tight and her heart painful as it clattered wildly. This was both sorrowful and humiliating, hearing Lady Clement speak so and with such clarity that it sounded as though it could not be denied, not even by the Duke himself!

"Please."

The soft way that the Duke spoke was the antithesis to the sharp voice of Lady Clement. Louisa dragged her gaze back to him, only to see that he was looking directly back at her, that word spoken to *her* rather than to the lady.

"Please," he said again, seeming to beg her with only a single word. Louisa knew what he was asking, heard what it was he was pleading to hear from her but she could not bring herself to say it. This time, there were no words she could offer Lady Clement to put her words to ruin, could not pretend that she had been with the Duke on the evening that he had supposedly been with Lady Clement. The trust that they had begun to build seemed to shatter as she shook her head, seeing the heaviness sink into the Duke's eyes as he gazed back at her, his shoulders dropping just a little.

Then, he took a breath.

"I want to hear no more of this, Lady Clement." He spoke firmly now, his chin lifted and, Louisa noticed, his hands curled into fists. "What you have said is a lie, for I was not with you on the evening that you said. I have not stepped into the arms of another ever since my engagement to Lady Louisa was announced and I stand firm by that. I do not know what it is – or who it is – that has driven you to say this but I will not stand for it. Do you understand?"

Lady Clement sniffed. "Say what you wish. I know the truth."

The Duke shook his head. "No, you speak lies. You are seeking to injure either myself or Lady Louisa or both of us, mayhap? But I can promise you now, Lady Clement, though I will not deny that we have been close together in previous times, I will never be so again. I will never come into your arms, never in your company again. I am committed solely to Lady Louisa and to her, that shall always be."

These words did nothing to bring Louisa's upset into any sort of calm. Instead, she turned her head away, looking blindly across to her left rather than looking at him. She did not know what to think. On the one hand, the Duke of Yarmouth was asking her to believe him, to trust him when she did not yet have full belief in his change of character though he had done a good deal to prove it to her. And yet, on the other hand, she had the fact that she had lied for him when it had been whispered that he had gone to the houses of disrepute – and what if she had been wrong? What if the Duke of Yarmouth *had* gone to one of those dark, illicit establishments and she had covered his true actions in lies? What if, thereafter, he was now seeking for her to lie for him again when, in fact, he *had* been in Lady Clement's company?

"That is disappointing to hear." Lady Clement sniffed, eyes narrowed now as Louisa forced herself to look back at the lady who had caused so much upset and pain. "I thought that, after all that you said to me, we might continue our connection and –"

"I have said I have heard enough, Lady Clement." The Duke's voice was hard now, anger burning through each word. "I do not think that you need to say anything more. Now," he continued, taking a small step towards Louisa, demanding her attention by the nearness of his presence. "I was eager to dance with you, Louisa. It is the waltz." There was a slight pause. "Will you dance with me?"

Louisa looked back at him with sad eyes, her heart thudding dully. What was she to say? To refuse him would be to say to all those near them – and to all those listening – that she did not believe he spoke the truth and that all that Lady Clement had said had broken her connection to the Duke. But to dance with him would give him the impression that she was contented to continue on just as they were when, in truth, she was not in the least bit certain about it all.

"I think you should, Louisa."

Lady Julia's voice murmured in her ear and heaving a sigh, Louisa took the Duke's hand and walked towards him, seeing the relief which poured into his expression though the concern in his eyes remained. They walked away from the small group, away from Lady Clement and yet, all the same, Louisa could feel the lady's eyes fixed to her back.

"Thank you, Louisa."

Her throat constricted. "Pray, do not speak to me, Your Grace."

"But it is not true!" he protested, urgently. "Please, I – "

"No." Louisa dropped her hand from his arm as they came to the dance floor, standing back from him so they might bow and curtsy to each other. "I will do what I must to get to the end of the evening without any further embarrassment, but thereafter, I do not know what I will do. Please, I cannot hear another word from you. It is too much." Her voice broke and she closed her eyes against the sudden rush of tears. "It is far too much."

When she opened her eyes, the Duke was looking at her with something akin to desperation in his eyes. The music began and he came close to her, one hand going to her waist, the other clasping her hand. He said nothing as they danced and Louisa concentrated solely on the steps, not letting herself think of anything other than that. She did not know how long they danced for, finding herself lost in sadness rather than any sort of happiness. When it came to a close, she stepped back as quickly as she could, before sinking into a curtsy.

"I am telling you the truth, Louisa," she heard him murmur, her eyes catching his gaze for just a moment. "And the truth is, I love you."

There was no joy in her heart, no springing up of happiness. Instead, Louisa simply looked at him before, after another moment, turned on her heel and walked away.

Chapter Nineteen

What am I to do?

Joseph clicked his fingers and within moments, another brandy was set before him. He took it and threw it back in two gulps before clicking his fingers again. Whites was quiet this evening and the footmen were quick to answer any of Joseph's requests, which he appreciated given his present mood.

"If you continue like that, then all will not be well."

Joseph looked up with bleary eyes, ruffling one hand through his hair. "I care not."

"Yes, you do." Lord Quillon sat down in the chair next to Joseph, taking the brandy from the footman before it could be handed to Joseph. "I think it best if I take that."

"Leave me be," Joseph muttered, looking away. "I need this." He felt as though everything within him was tangled up in knots, knots that he had no hope of untying. Letting out a long, harsh breath, he shook his head. "I am lost."

Lord Quillon nodded. "Yes, I heard about Lady Clement."

"You did?" Joseph rolled his eyes. "No doubt all of the *ton* was abuzz with the news before I quit the ball." He let out a slow breath, pain lancing his chest. "How glad I am that Lady Louisa returned home shortly after our dance. I do not think that it would have been good for her to remain, to hear what was being said."

His friend eyed him for a few moments, then tipped his head, one eyebrow lifting. "Is it true?"

Another strike of pain hit him. "No, it is not."

Lord Quillon took in a deep breath. "Very well. Then what are you going to do about it?"

Joseph blinked. "Do?"

"Yes, what are you going to do?" Lord Quillon smiled lightly, shrugging his shoulders. "What is it that *you* are going to do when it comes to your betrothed and Lady Clement?"

Closing his eyes, Joseph let out a heavy breath. "I do not know, though I must tell you that I appreciate your trust in my words. That is a little unexpected."

Saying nothing, Lord Quillon took a sip of Joseph's brandy, his question remaining unanswered.

"I do not think there is anything that I *can* do," Joseph continued, after a few moments of silence. "I asked Lady Louisa to dance with me and she did, only to tell me that she could not hear another word from my lips." This time, when pain struck him, it was with such force that he snatched in a breath – and Lord Quillon noticed it. Closing his eyes so as to hide the question he saw in his friend's eyes, Joseph shook his head. "I can do nothing."

"But it is not true," Lord Quillon countered. "There must be a way to prove that you were not with her, as she says, surely?"

"It is not about that!" Getting to his feet, Joseph strode towards the fireplace and then back again, pushing both hands through his hair this time. "I do not care what society thinks of me, truth be told! The only person that matters is Louisa and she does not believe me, not even when I – " Stopping dead, he let out a harsh breath and then flopped down into his chair with a groan. "Not even when I tell her that I love her."

The silence that met him was like an insurmountable wall. Joseph sat forward, his elbows on his knees and his hands pushed through his hair, not willing, not *able,* to look back at his friend. What he had said to Lady Louisa had come from a place so deep within himself, he had barely been able to recognize it but yet, he knew those words to be true. He *had* fallen for her in a way that he had never even imagined could be, had found her so remarkable, so wonderful and determined that he had lost his heart to her completely – and had only acknowledged it when he had been given no other choice. Part of him had hoped that she would believe what he had said, would rush into his arms and confess the same but, instead, she had turned around and walked away, leaving him feeling empty and alone.

Those feelings had not gone.

"I did not ever think it would be but I can tell by your demeanour that you are lost in love," Lord Quillon said, quietly. "Goodness, I cannot imagine what you must be feeling at present."

"Broken." Joseph swept one hand across his eyes and then looked back at Lord Quillon. "I do not understand why Lady Clement is saying such a thing! She is speaking such great untruths that they are injuring both Louisa and myself – and it is Louisa that I am concerned about the most. I think... I think this has shattered what we were building together and I do not know what to do."

"I wish I could advise." After a moment, Lord Quillon beckoned to the footman who then brought over two brandies, one for Joseph and one for Lord Quillon. Taking it, Lord Quillon returned his attention back to Joseph, having clearly been thinking in these last few minutes. "The only thing I can suggest is that you somehow find out who has encouraged Lady Clement to speak lies to the *ton*. Clearly, this was purposeful."

Something rushed back into Joseph's mind with such force, Joseph stared back at his friend, feeling as though his heart had stopped dead. It was only when Lord Quillon cleared his throat that Joseph finally spoke, a slight tremor running through him. "Louisa... she – she received a letter from someone anonymous, informing her that they were determined to do whatever was necessary to encourage her father to end the engagement."

Lord Quillon let out a long, exasperated breath. "And you did not think to tell me this before now?"

"I only just recalled it. With everything that has happened, I quite forgot. Yes, *yes*, of course! This must be connected!"

"I should think so." Lord Quillon smiled quickly. "And should Lady Louisa be reminded of that letter, it is possible she might draw the connection. She might then be more inclined to believe that you are telling her the truth."

Joseph rubbed one hand over his chin, thinking quickly. "Yes, I suppose that could help, though I do not think that she wants to speak with me at present."

Lord Quillon sat forward in his chair. "I can help with that. Let me speak about this all to Lady Julia. She is fiercely loyal to Lady Louisa, of course, but she is also very level headed. She will listen to what I have to say and might be willing to do what she can to help you. I know that she wants Lady Louisa to find happiness and I do believe that she was beginning to think it might come from her connection to you."

Joseph's heart surged with hope. "That is what I want also."

"Then you truly do love her?" Lord Quillon searched Joseph's face, as though trying to ascertain whether Joseph was being entirely truthful. "You want this for *her* best, not for yours?"

"With my whole heart," Joseph answered, spreading out his hands wide. "I have felt something for the lady for some time, though I have ignored it, determined that I would not permit myself to have any sort of affection for her."

"Why not?"

It was a difficult question to answer but Joseph did his utmost to be honest. "That is a question I have fought through." Sighing, he sat back in his seat, his gaze to the left of Lord Quillon. "I believe, loathe though I am to admit it, that I was afraid."

Lord Quillon's eyebrows shot up.

"Afraid of what I did not know," Joseph continued, the words coming more quickly now. "I had always pushed aside the notion of love and thus, when it began to creep upon me, I pushed it away. I did not want it, I told myself. Though when I saw the pain in Louisa's eyes, when I saw her step back from me instead of towards me, I finally realized the truth."

"And what was that?"

Letting out a slow breath, Joseph lifted his shoulders and then let them drop. "That I wanted her to step into my arms, to declare that she trusted me wholeheartedly and knew that I cared for her so deeply, I would never do something so grievous to her. That was what I wanted – and I wanted to be that *for* her." His heart squeezed hard. "And instead, I had precisely the opposite."

His friend nodded slowly. "Well, if that is what you have learned about yourself, then I think it only right that you do everything you can to pursue it, to heal the rift between Lady Louisa and yourself, so that you might have what you hope for."

Taking in a deep breath, Joseph set his shoulders back. There were things he could do, things he could threaten that would make Lady Clement speak, he realized. It was not something he wished to do but, as Lord Quillon had said, he had to do everything he could to pursue Lady Louisa's heart again. "Yes, you are quite correct, I *do* need to do so. And I shall... and I will begin by speaking directly to Lady Clement."

***

"My dear Yarmouth, there is no need for you to stand outside my carriage!" Lady Clement's smile was bright, her eyes beckoning him towards her. "You know as well as I just how often you have sat with me in here."

"But I shall not today," Joseph answered, firmly. "I thought you would come to Hyde Park for the fashionable hour and I am determined now to speak with you."

She tilted her head, her eyes flashing as she studied him from where she sat in her carriage, the door open. "But you are insisting that I come out of my carriage to join you, rather than doing what you ought and coming to join *me*."

"I have no time for games!" Joseph squeezed his hands tight closed, determined not to lose his temper. "Please. There is much at stake here, though you either do not know of it – or if you do, then you do not care about it. But it means a great deal to me."

Lady Clement's gaze sharpened. "This is about your betrothal."

Joseph lifted his chin, thinking now that he would do whatever he could to remove Lady Clement from the carriage so they might speak together, rather that practically shouting at one another. She had to know that he was not going to be playful, teasing or jovial over this. It was nothing but serious. "Lady Clement, I insist that you come to join me – and you will do so, unless you would prefer that I take what I know of your *other* liaisons and speak of them to the *ton*, just as you have spoken to them of our connection." It was not a kind thing to say, he knew, and his conscience pricked him but, all the same, it had the desired effect. Lady Clement's eyes widened, her face drained of color and, within a few moments, she was standing beside him on the grass.

"How dare you threaten me in such a way?" she hissed, a hint of red beginning to snake up into her cheeks. "You know that you cannot speak of such things!"

Joseph leaned a little closer. "And yet, *you* can say whatever you wish and ruin my happiness?"

"Happiness?" Lady Clement reared back, her eyes filled with confusion. "Whatever are you speaking of? You are not engaged to Lady Louisa out of anything other than requirement and nor is she engaged to you out of affection! You cannot pretend otherwise."

"I love her."

Joseph waited until what he had said had taken a hold of Lady Clement, watching her eyes round, the color fading from her face again. She said nothing for some moments, studying him, clearly uncertain as to whether she ought to believe him or not.

"My goodness." She tilted her head. "I do not think that I have ever been more disappointed."

"Disappointed?"

Lady Clement nodded, perhaps seeing Joseph's surprise. "I thought that we might truly come back together again, that you were just as much of a rogue as you have ever been."

"I am afraid I am not." Joseph took in a breath, then spoke with as much firmness as he could. "I *must* know who told you to speak as you did, Lady Clement. There was no truth in what you said and yet, you determined to do it. Someone begged it of you, someone insisted that you do such a thing and I must know who it was."

Lady Clement's chin jutted forward. "I do not know of what you are speaking."

"Yes, you do." Joseph came closer to her again, aware that there were many people around them but having such a strong desire to hear the truth from her, he did not care what they thought. "Do you not see what you have done, Lady Clement? I have found myself entirely altered ever since I met Lady Louisa. I want to be the very best sort of gentleman I can be, simply so that *she* can find the greatest amount of happiness possible. I am well aware that I have no greatness about my character, that I do not deserve to have such a beautiful and kind young lady by my side as my wife but that is the situation that has been given to me and I fully intend to keep a hold of it."

Lady Clement's eyes flickered. "Because you love her."

"Yes." Something tightened in Joseph's throat but he held her gaze steadily. "Yes, it is because I have fallen in love with her – and because I fear that your words and your untruths spoken so boldly in front of her but also to the *ton* will rend our connection useless and broken. What if her father now determines that the engagement can and should be broken? What if I am no longer able to call her my betrothed?" A flood of fear washed over him and he took another step closer, a slight trembling in his frame. "What then, Lady Clement? What shall I do?"

The lady blinked rapidly, put one hand to his arm and then released it only a second later, as though he had burned her fingers somehow. "I – I did not realise... I was told that – "

"What were you told?"

Lady Clement closed her eyes and then shook her head. "I was told that Lady Louisa was in a situation of great difficulty, that she did not want to be wed but had no other choice in the matter."

"And you decided to do as was asked of you out of concern for her?" Joseph asked, quite certain that this could *not* be the case. "That does not sound in the least bit like something you would do."

A hint of a smile touched the edge of Lady Clement's lips. "That is because it is not. You know me well enough there!"

"Then why did you do it."

She closed her eyes. "Because, like you, this lady knew of my connection to some other gentlemen of the *ton.* She threatened to reveal one or two of them to select members of society, knowing that my reputation would be utterly ruined, should she do so. However," she continued, a breath of relief escaping her, "that threat has now passed, for I have done what was required of me and there can be no more need for my assistance."

Joseph's heart began to quicken, his hands clenching and unclenching. "A name," he said, a little hoarsely. "I need to know who it was, Lady Clement, *please.*"

Her lips twisted, her eyes darting away.

"I will not say or do anything further to upset you," Joseph promised, quickly. "This lady, whoever she is, has the misguided impression that Lady Louisa is unhappy in her match. That might have been so at one point but it is not now."

Lady Clement's eyebrows lifted. "You mean to say that she loves you too?"

Joseph's heart tore. "Would that I could say it was so, but no," he answered, a little more quietly. "She is not unhappy, however, has no desire to end our betrothal – or, at the very least, she *did* not. I must pray that that will not have changed."

Lady Clement closed her eyes, shook her head and let out

another long, slow breath. "Hannah. Lady Hannah."

Dizziness rushed over him as Joseph closed his eyes, his heart sinking low. Why had he never thought of her before? The lady who had been so upset by his treatment of her friend, the one who had spoken so harshly – albeit fairly – to him at the very start of the Season, *she* was the one doing what she could for Lady Louisa! That made a good deal of sense, Joseph considered, going weak with relief as he opened his eyes again and then looked back at Lady Clement. "Thank you."

She nodded though there was something in her eyes he could not make out. Sadness, mayhap? Regret or envy? "Good afternoon, Your Grace."

Joseph inclined his head. "Goodbye, Lady Clement." It was a farewell, a parting of their ways, with the quiet, whispering promise that he would never again return to her company. Turning on his heel, Joseph strode back towards his own carriage, determined now to make his way directly towards Lady Louisa's townhouse. He *had* to find her, had to speak with her just as soon as he could, had to pray that she would listen to him. His heart demanded nothing less.

Chapter Twenty

"Lord Proudfoot has asked Father for his permission to court me!"

Louisa looked up from where she had been attempting to read, though she had not taken in a single word ever since she had opened the book. "Lord Proudfoot?"

"Yes!" Rachel twirled around the room, her eyes bright. "And Lord Sibminster has only just now gone to speak with father about courting Ruth!"

"Lord Sibminster?" Louisa repeated, setting her book aside and then rising to her feet. "The Earl? I know he has danced a great deal with you both and come to take tea only once but I did not think that he had any real interest."

"But he does!" Rachel came towards her and then caught her hands, whirling Louisa around. "And Ruth is quite taken with him also, just as I am with Lord Proudfoot! Is that not wonderful?"

Louisa nodded and tried to smile. "Yes, of course it is," she murmured, taking her hands away from her sister as she stood quietly rather than dancing around the room. "I am truly delighted for you both."

The door opened and closed and Ruth came in, smiling gently. "You have been told the news, then?" A good deal more demure than Rachel, Ruth smiled and came closer to Louisa, reaching to take one of Louisa's hands and squeezing it for a moment. "I am very happy indeed at his offer of courtship."

"That is good." Louisa took in a deep breath and then let it out as surreptitiously as she could, fighting back the sudden rush of tears, wishing that she could have been as happy as her sister from the very first moment she had been in company with the Duke. The brief happiness and hope she had permitted to enter her heart had gone now, lost in the darkness which had followed Lady Clement's revelation.

"Are you quite all right?" Ruth came a little closer, though Rachel went to ring the bell for tea, clearly not in the least bit concerned about Louisa's present state of mind. "I know that you must be upset about what was said, but I am also certain that you will have absolute clarity about it."

A frown pulled at Louisa's forehead. "Clarity?"

"Yes." Ruth offered her a small shrug. "That letter you received, yes? It must be the reason behind Lady Clement speaking as she did."

The room itself seemed to tilt as Louisa was reminded, with great swiftness, that she had received a note from an anonymous lady, seeming to promise her that she would do whatever she could to encourage Louisa's father to end the engagement. Why had she not thought of that? "Do... do you think the two could be connected, Ruth?" Her voice was unsteady as she felt, a slight break in her words given the strength of her sudden emotion. "Lady Clement was very convincing and —"

"But you do not believe her, surely?" Ruth's eyes rounded at the edges. "It all seemed rather convenient, do you not think? The way she came up to the Duke and yourself, announcing in a loud voice that they had not only shared a previous connection but had been in each other's company very recently indeed. Why would a lady such as herself do that?"

Louisa blinked rapidly, her heart beginning to quail. Had she made a dreadful misjudgment here? "I thought that she would have said such a thing because of her desire for the Duke."

"But that would not do!" Ruth exclaimed, coming to take Louisa's hand, perhaps seeing the anguish now which Louisa felt spreading out across her heart and up into her chest. "What purpose would there be in spreading news of her time with the Duke through all of London? That would damage her own reputation, even though she might well be known for that, and it certainly would do nothing to draw the Duke back towards her! Think about it, Louisa!" Ruth gazed into Louisa's eyes for a moment, her hand squeezing Louisa's. "Lady Clement stated that she had been in company with the Duke of Yarmouth only a few days ago. In speaking as she did, in revealing her connection to him to all of society, she would only *damage* that connection, rather than improve it! If it *was* true that she had that closeness with the Duke, then to speak so boldly would risk ending that, would it not?"

Putting one hand to her forehead, a chill running through her, Louisa closed her eyes. "I did not think of that."

"You believed her, then."

"I – I did not know what to believe," Louisa answered, a little weakly. "I thought that there must be truth to it, given the way that she spoke."

Ruth's eyes flickered with what Louisa took to be anger, though not directed at her. "Lady Clement spoke with determination and boldness, yes and I can see why some might be convinced by her, but surely you have enough wisdom now to realise that it could not have been the truth! And couple that with the letter you received, then is it not possible that the letter writer is the reason that Lady Clement spoke so?"

Louisa's hand dropped to her side and, feeling weak, she sank down into her chair. This appeared to catch even Rachel's attention and she came over to join them both, her eyes filled with a sudden concern.

"You ought not to believe a word that Lady Clement said," Ruth told her, decisively, though she too came to sit down. "I am certain that it was a ploy to end your connection to the Duke once and for all – just as the letter writer said they would do."

"Because they think they are saving me from an engagement I do not want," Louisa whispered, a single tear dropping to her cheek. "Goodness, why did I ever think that there was truth to this? I stepped away from the Duke, I told him that I did not want to hear another word from him when, in fact, he was telling the truth."

Her sisters fell silent for a moment, glancing at each other.

"I do not think that you should blame yourself." This time, it was Rachel who spoke up, rather than Ruth. "We all know the reputation of the Duke of Yarmouth, so it is to be expected that something like that might well have brought your doubts to the fore."

"And Lady Clement *was* very convincing." Ruth smiled briefly, just as the maid knocked at the door, no doubt with the tea tray. "But I would be inclined to believe that the Duke of Yarmouth was telling you the truth. He was not in her company, he was not with her from one evening to the following morning. It appears, my dear sister, that he has been loyal to you."

"Just as he said he wished to be," Louisa whispered, closing her eyes against a sudden torrent of tears. "Oh, what have I done?"

"It was Lady Hannah."

Louisa's head shot up, her breath catching in her throat as the Duke rushed towards her, his eyes rounded and fixed to hers. "Your... Your Grace!"

"Please, if you would come with me, I would like to call upon Lady Hannah this moment," he said, holding one hand out to her. "Please, Louisa, come with me."

Louisa swallowed tightly. "I cannot," she rasped, aware of her need to be in the company of her sisters as gentlemen came to call. "I – "

"We will have the maid *and* father can come to do his duty, just as he ought," Rachel interrupted, firmly. "You should go with the Duke. Go now."

Ruth put one hand to the small of Louisa's back, urging her forward. "Go. Take another maid with you if you wish but I think you ought to do as is asked of you."

The Duke said nothing, his gaze melded to hers and the slight flicker of hope in his eyes made Louisa's heart break. How much she had pained him with her distrust!

"You think it was Lady Hannah?" she asked, taking a single step towards him as he nodded fervently. "Why?"

"I spoke to Lady Clement at length. I spoke to her in Hyde Park. I did not climb into her carriage but I insisted that she come and speak with me," he told her, his hand still outstretched. "The *ton* saw me, no doubt, but I do not care. I had to hear the truth from her and hear it, I did."

"And she told you this?" Louisa blinked, a little confused. "Why did she speak so openly to you?"

The Duke pressed his lips together. "I did not like to do it, but I threatened to expose some of her connections to the *ton*. As it turns out, that was the very same threat that was made to her by Lady Hannah."

Louisa closed her eyes, breathing hard as she took in all that had been said. "Why would Lady Hannah do such a thing?"

"Let us go and ask her."

Opening her eyes, Louisa took in the Duke's outstretched hand, then let her gaze go to his face. His expression was one of tormented hope, his face drawn, eyes a little darker than usual, his mouth pulled tight as though he was anticipating her refusal.

"Very well."

The Duke's eyes flared.

"I will go with you," she said, softly. "And I will hear what Lady Hannah has to say." She trembled as her fingers wrapped around his hand, his heart threatening to leap up into her chest, though she quietened it with an effort.

"Thank you, Louisa." Without warning, the Duke lowered his head, lifted their joined hands and pressed a kiss to the back of her hand. "You cannot know what this means to me. It is the only chance I have to prove to you that I am not what you might think of me, not any longer. I have changed, I have altered completely – and it is all because of you."

Louisa said nothing, though her whole body slowly began to warm. Without so much as a backwards glance towards her sisters, she walked out of the room beside the Duke, her hand still in his and with hope beginning to grow with every step she took.

Chapter Twenty-One

"We must speak with Lady Hannah." Joseph cleared his throat. "Now."

He glanced to where Lady Louisa was grasping his arm, glad that she stood with him at least, though she had said nothing to him in the carriage ride. She had not even paused to call for a maid and that, Joseph considered, had been a good thing for it meant that she was urgent in her desire to hear what Lady Hannah had to say. His chest grew tight as they waited for the butler's return, hoping that they would be given the chance for an audience with Lady Hannah that afternoon. He did not think that he could wait until another time, not when Lady Louisa had been so willing to come with him. This was his one moment with her, his one chance, he felt, for her to learn the truth. A truth he *had* to cling onto in the hope that she might finally believe him and accept *all* that he wanted to tell her.

"Lady Hannah and her mother, Lady Wigton, will see you in the drawing room."

Joseph nodded, glanced again to Lady Louisa but then followed after the butler without a word, his heart picking up speed as he walked. Pressing his lips tight together, he bowed low before the two ladies, though, he noted, Lady Hannah's face was rather pale, her gaze darting from himself to Lady Louisa and back again.

"Good afternoon, Your Grace, Lady Louisa." Lady Wigton gestured for them both to sit down though Joseph could see the confusion in her expression. "How unexpected it is to have you both call."

"There is a purpose in our visit, Lady Wigton," Joseph began, though Lady Louisa's hand tightened on his arm and he looked to her, a little uncertain as to why she had squeezed his arm so. Was it that she wished to silence him? And if so, for what purpose?

"I shall ring for tea, Mama." Lady Hannah rose quickly and did as she had said, but Joseph kept his gaze upon her as she returned to her seat. The lady, however, did not look back at him as he might have expected. Instead, her head bent forward, her gaze fell low and she licked her lips, clearly a little ill at ease. Joseph waited until Lady Louisa had taken a seat before he also sat down, choosing the chair that was as close to his betrothed as he could. He wanted to be very near to her indeed, as though this might be the very last moment he was in her company.

"Well, now." Lady Wigton smiled but it did not linger. "Might I ask if –"

"I received your letter, Lady Hannah."

Joseph's skin prickled as Lady Louisa spoke up, throwing an apologetic look towards Lady Wigton for the interruption. He remained where he was, just as a scratch came to the door with the maid coming in with the tea tray. It was set out in silence, for the conversation immediately came to a close so that the servant would not overhear anything and then gossip about it as the servants were so often inclined to do. Taking the opportunity to study Lady Hannah's expression, Joseph's eyebrows lifted in surprise. Lady Hannah had gone very pale indeed, her eyes rounded and fixed to Lady Louisa's, her hands gripping the arms of the chair.

She knows what is being spoken of, Joseph thought to himself, hope beginning to rise in his chest. *Lady Louisa too, she must know now that Lady Hannah sent the note!*

It had not been something that either of them had mentioned on their carriage ride over to Lady Hannah's abode but it seemed now that Lady Louisa had done a good deal of thinking in their time apart. Perhaps she had already come to the same realization as he – though she had not yet said anything.

"Letter?" Lady Wigton frowned, then waved one hand in her daughter's direction. "Hannah, might you pour the tea? Goodness, this is the future Duchess of Yarmouth! She will think you dreadfully rude, I am sure!"

"No, I do not, not in the least." Lady Louisa smiled and Joseph let out a slow, surreptitious breath, his heart beginning to free itself of all the tension that he had wound around it. "Although I would certainly enjoy a cup of tea." She smiled and Joseph swallowed tightly, seeing the beauty of both her face and her character shining through. She was gentle in her approach, considerate and kind and Joseph marveled at her. This was not what he wanted to do. Truth be told, he wanted to rail at Lady Hannah, to demand with both fury and upset in his voice, that she told them everything, heedless to the fright he might cause her. But Lady Louisa was the utter opposite of him. She was the opposite of him in every way, Joseph considered, and that was the beauty of her. How little he deserved having such a sweetness beside him! And how grateful he was for all that she brought, offered and gave to him.

"Thank you." He took the tea cup from Lady Hannah, noticing the slight tremble in her fingers. Joseph glanced up at the lady but she had already stepped back, leaving him to catch Lady Louisa's eye. She was not smiling but gave him a small nod, as though to say that she knew what had to be said, what had to be done and would be willing to do it.

"Lady Wigton," she began, her voice soft. "Might I be so bold as to ask for a few minutes alone with Lady Hannah? There is a private matter that I wish to discuss with her and, you can understand, I can only really speak freely if we have no other company. I can assure you, it will only be for a few minutes and we would both be very much in your debt." A sidelong glance towards Joseph from Lady Louisa told him that she needed him to lay emphasis on this and, quickly, Joseph did so.

"We would be very much in your debt," he said, seeing the surprise leap into Lady Wigton's expression. "It is a strange request, I am sure, but we would not ask unless it was important."

"And it is *very* important." Lady Louisa smiled but lifted her eyebrows expectantly and, much to Joseph's relief, Lady Wigton gave her consent, albeit in a somewhat flustered manner.

"This is most extraordinary, I must say," she began, shaking her head but then rising to her feet. "Hannah? Do you know what this matter is about?"

Lady Hannah swallowed. "Yes, Mama, I believe I do. I am happy to speak with Lady Louisa."

Lady Wigton cleared her throat, clasping her hands in front of her. "Very well, I shall take my leave, though I would like to know something about what is to be discussed, if you please? I do hope that my daughter will not suffer any consequences from this."

Joseph shook his head. "No, of course not."

"Indeed not," Lady Louisa added. "It is only about a lady of the *ton* whom both Lady Hannah and myself are acquainted with. I have heard something about her and wish to clarify as to whether or not Lady Hannah has heard the same. I must be very careful about my reputation, given that I am soon to be a Duchess, but at the same time, I do not want to speak falsehoods as though they were truths! That is why I ask for some privacy. I am sure that you understand, Lady Wigton, for you are always full of wisdom."

This seemed to satisfy Lady Wigton, for a hint of a smile drew itself across her mouth and, with a nod, she stepped out of the room.

Silence fell.

Joseph turned his attention back towards Lady Hannah, noting how the lady began to smooth out her dress, her head lowered, her gaze pinned to her hands rather than looking at either of them.

"You sent Louisa a letter, Lady Hannah," Joseph began, doing his best to keep his voice calm and quiet. "You seek to end the betrothal between us, I think."

Lady Hannah's frame grew tight. "I did not want you to marry her."

"Because you knew that I had no choice in the matter," Lady Louisa said, gently. "You believed that my father consented, being either unaware of the Duke's reputation or being heedless to it."

Lady Hannah finally lifted her head. "I know what he did to my *dear* friend, Lady Sara," she said, as though Joseph was not in the room. "I could not bear to think of you suffering in a marriage to him! We are not very well known to each other, yes, but we are acquainted enough for me to know that you are kind, selfless and good-hearted – the very opposite of the Duke of Yarmouth! I found out that the engagement came about through the Duchess of Yarmouth approaching your father and, given what I know of your father, I thought I would do what I could to encourage *him* to be the one to end the betrothal. I did not think that you would be able to do so without his consent."

Lady Louisa closed her eyes briefly, though she did smile.

"You are most considerate, Lady Hannah."

"Nor did I want him to have the happiness that he denied so many others," Lady Hannah continued, her voice breaking now. "It did not seem right."

"That is because it is not right nor fair," Joseph interrupted, forcing both ladies to turn to him. He closed his eyes for a moment, the weight of his past sins coming to sit heavily upon his chest. "You are quite right in all that you have said, Lady Hannah. None of what I have done in the past was good or right. To have been given the gift of Lady Louisa's hand in mine is something that I certainly do *not* deserve and I will fully admit to that." Pausing for a moment, he spread out his hands either side. "I do not know what else to say to you but to apologise for the pain, the sorrow and the anguish that I caused to so many, including to your friend, Lady Sara. I have told Lady Louisa that I want to change, that I wish to alter my character so that I might become the very best gentleman in all of England – in all of the world, if that were possible – and that is because of what I have seen in her. I do not think I shall ever deserve her, do not believe that I shall ever be good enough to have her by my side and that is something I shall bear all of my days. A consequence, mayhap, of all that I have done but it is a weight I shall bear willingly."

Lady Hannah's eyes widened just a fraction, though she then quickly frowned. "I – I do not know whether I can believe you."

"You can."

Joseph's heart trembled as he looked to Lady Louisa. She was looking up at him, her eyes shining, her lips in a soft smile. He could not speak, such was the tightness in his throat, but his joy exploded through him all the same.

"You told Lady Clement to speak those lies to the Duke and to the *ton*?" Lady Louisa continued, still in a gentle tone. "You spread rumours about the Duke too?"

Lady Hannah closed her eyes and a single tear fell to her cheek. "I will admit that I did. I hoped that one of the rumours would be enough to have Lord Jedburgh tell you to end the engagement but when it did not, I chose to speak to Lady Clement. I knew of her liaisons – it does not matter how – but I also was aware that some of them held great shame for her. I am sorry if I injured you in the process, Lady Louisa." Her voice shaking now, Lady Hannah sniffed once, twice, and then opened her eyes, reaching to take Lady Louisa's hand. "I wanted to protect you, knowing all that you had done and all that you had given up for your sisters."

"How very kind of you to think so of me." Lady Louisa leaned a little closer to Lady Hannah, clearly wanting to reassure her. "I will admit, I did not want to marry the Duke of Yarmouth. However, now with the time that we have spent together and the changes I have seen in him, I confess that my heart now fully desires to be with him. Do not think that I have come to berate you or to demand your confession in front of the *ton*, for that is not something that I either would do or would desire. All I want now is to thank you for your consideration of me, to tell you that I do value your concern – but also to ask you now to desist."

Lady Hannah nodded, her gaze falling to the floor.

"I think I shall be quite contented with the Duke of Yarmouth," Lady Louisa continued, though her gaze swung to Joseph, a sweetness there that he had never expected to see. "We shall be very happily married, I am sure."

Epilogue

"Did you mean those words?"

The carriage rumbled back towards Lady Louisa's townhouse, though Joseph had already directed the driver to take the longest route he could think of, wanting to spend as much time alone with his betrothed as he could.

Lady Louisa smiled at him. "I did." Her smile faded for just a moment, her hand reaching to take his as they sat opposite each other in the carriage. "I am sorry I did not believe you, Yarmouth. I should have thought of the letter, I should have realised that there was more to Lady Clement's words. I did not think. All I saw was the breaking of our connection... and of my heart."

"I do not blame you, not in the least." Shifting quickly so that he could sit beside Lady Louisa, Joseph kept her hand tight in his as she turned to look up at him. "I am precisely who Lady Hannah believed me to be. There was no reason for you to trust me, no reason why I would not have done as Lady Clement said. All you had was my word and that did not have any great strength with it!"

Lady Louisa sighed quietly. "All the same, I knew that you were changing into a trustworthy fellow. I knew that we had shared a good deal thus far, that you had proven to me you were not as the rumours had said. I did have a trust in you – a trust that was far too easily shattered when Lady Clement spoke." She closed her eyes. "I am sorry for turning away from you when you told me those words."

For a moment, Joseph did not understand what she meant. It was only when she looked up at him again, hope flickering there, that he realized. "When I told you that I loved you?"

She nodded, her fingers twining through his. "Is that true?"

Joseph smiled. "Is it true that I love you?" Lifting her hand to his mouth, he kissed it gently. "Louisa, I have been broken apart by what I feel for you. I wanted to turn away from it at one point, wanted to pretend that I did not feel it, that it was not important to me – only now to realise that it is the only thing of value that I have! My heart cried out with pain and sadness when we were apart, my whole being tight with fear at the thought of losing you from my arms. Yes, Louisa, I love you though I do not deserve to have even a minute of your company. I know. I will continue to love you with all of my heart and with all of myself, in the hope that one day, I might be worthy of you."

When she smiled, it was as though the clouds had all blown away and the sun shone so brightly, it seared the air around him. When she tilted her head up and kissed him, it was as if the sunshine pierced his heart, filling him with light. Wrapping his arms around her as best he could, Joseph gave in to all that he felt, wishing and praying and hoping that, somehow, he might be able to convey the love he had for her.

"I love you too, Yarmouth." Breaking the kiss, Lady Louisa whispered those wonderful words against his lips, her eyes still closed. "The sadness that I felt, the unbearable ache in my heart when I thought we were separated by lies and deceit told me that I felt more for you than I had ever permitted myself to believe – until I realised that it was nothing but love."

Framing her face with his hands, Joseph looked down into her eyes, hardly able to believe that she had offered him something so wonderful. "I will love you until my dying day," he promised, every word fervent. "And I will be committed to you with all of my heart. I swear it to you now as I shall swear it to you on our wedding day."

She smiled, her eyes flickering closed. "Then kiss me again, Yarmouth, and seal those words with your lips."

And Joseph could do nothing but oblige her.

THE END

Printed in Great Britain
by Amazon